Murder Under the Midnight Sun

This book has been translated with financial support
from:

 **ICELANDIC LITERATURE CENTER**

Published by agreement with Forlagið
www.forlagid.is

Corylus Books Ltd

corylusbooks.com

ISBN: 978-1-7392989-4-4

Murder Under the Midnight Sun

Stella Blómkvist

Translated by Quentin Bates

Published by Corylus Books Ltd

1

Wednesday 2nd June 2010

Wow!

A little guy in rich man's clothes. A proper Tom Thumb.
Or something like that.

To be fair, he's not exactly a midget. He has to be around one metre sixty in height.

He's wearing a ruinously expensive pinstriped suit, complete with matching waistcoat. There's a sky-blue silk tie knotted at his throat. He has a neat beard, flecked with grey. His thick, grey hair is combed straight back.

This dapper Brit's name is Gregory George MacKenzie.

He sent me a registered letter from London a week ago, a formal invitation to lunch at Hótel Holt in Reykjavík, to discuss an urgent and lucrative opportunity.

There was a detailed résumé in the same envelope. According to this, he's a British businessman in his sixties. Scottish ancestry, resident in London.

MacKenzie sips a glass of dark port at the bar in this temple of wealth and culture as I come in from the sunshine that bathes the old houses of the Thingholt district.

He puts the glass down. A handshake, head bowed for a moment like an English aristocrat in an old movie. Then he calls the waiter, who shows us to the hotel's Kjarval room. This is where giant daubs by an eccentric dead painter hang on the walls.

It's art that reeks of money long after the artist's dead.

The two of us sit at a round table.

He's already ordered for both of us. Pan-fried duck liver as a starter. Grilled langoustine, still in their shells, as the main. Crème brûlée to finish up.

This is clearly a man who knows what he wants. And he's used to getting his own way.

MacKenzie chats expansively about himself as we work our way through the exquisite courses.

'My father had a shop in Glasgow when I was growing up,' he says. 'I worked behind the counter as a youngster and even while I was studying at the London School of Economics. I graduated and had job offers from city companies, including one of the biggest investment banks, but my father was adamant that I take over the family business. I was reluctant, but finally agreed to take over for a year, on condition that I could make all the changes I wanted. He accepted that. In a few weeks, I totally revamped the shop, brought it bang up to date. When that year came to an end, the shop had made a healthy profit and I opened another one exactly the same in a different district of Glasgow and a third in Edinburgh. That one year I expected to run the family shop turned into thirty-six, and 223 shops in five countries.'

'Cheers to that!'

He nods, raising his glass of red wine.

'Business has been my absolute life-long priority,' he continues. 'I found out when I was around thirty that I couldn't have children, and it was something of a relief at the time, because I didn't feel I had time for family life. Nature was kinder to my sister Muriel, who bore a daughter – outside wedlock, unfortunately – whose 29th birthday is today.'

'What does she do?' I ask, purely to be polite.

MacKenzie puts down his spoon.

'That's the big question,' he says.

'Meaning what?'

'Julia MacKenzie was twenty years old in 2001. She was studying geology at Edinburgh University and decided to take a trip to Iceland to see the volcanoes, mudpots and hot springs. She took the ferry from Scotland to the Faroe Islands, and from there to Iceland. She had been travelling around on her motorcycle for fifteen or sixteen days when she disappeared.'

'Disappeared, how?'

'I have no idea, because the investigation by the Icelandic police yielded no results. The police couldn't find her or the bike, and concluded that she'd become the victim of an accident in some unidentified place, under unknown circumstances. It was as if she'd vanished into thin air.'

MacKenzie breathes deeply the aroma of cognac in his balloon glass.

'I've been to Iceland once before,' he continues. 'I came here to collect my sister when the police gave up on an organised search for her daughter. Muriel was a broken woman, and has never recovered from the shock.'

He puts his glass aside.

'And that brings me to the business of the day,' he says. 'Four months ago my sister was diagnosed with terminal cancer. She begged me to make one last attempt to find out what happened to her daughter in Iceland. I tasked my lawyers in London with finding a suitable person in Iceland with experience of resolving cases that have long gone cold. They came to the unanimous conclusion that you're the most likely Icelandic lawyer to be successful, and the least likely to give up on what looks to be a hopeless task.'

'I never give up.'

'That's good to hear.'

'A lot of people have disappeared without trace here over the last few decades,' I add. 'Iceland is a sparsely populated place. Most of the country is mountainous Highlands, and nobody lives there permanently. That's because it's pretty much a desert. Nothing but glaciers, volcanoes, lava, boulders and rocks. It's dangerous territory and easy for someone unfamiliar with the conditions to come to grief.'

'I'm fully aware of that.'

The old guy picks up a dark blue document case from the floor and places it on a chair at his side.

'Over the last few months my staff have gathered every available piece of information relating to my niece's travels to Iceland and the search for her. It's all in this case. According to this, she was not in the Highlands when she disappeared, as the last recorded transaction on her bank card was at a filling station on the main road. She wasn't out in the wilderness, which makes her disappearance even more mystifying.'

'I see.'

'My wish is that you take all this information, examine it carefully, and discuss it with the people who were in charge of the search nine years ago. My hope is that you could discover something new, or find some clue in the documentation or discussions with these people that could give an indication of what became of my niece.'

'I can't promise any results,' I reply. 'To be completely honest with you, it's unlikely that I'll find anything significant that the search co-ordinators would've missed back then.'

'It's of the utmost importance to me to do everything I can

to fulfil my sister's final wish, if that's possible. I'll pay whatever you ask.'

'I see.'

'There are five million Icelandic krónur in the case, in cash. Please treat this as an advance payment for costs incurred and your time.'

Costs? Time? For having lunch at Hótel Holt?

Sometimes an offer is simply too good to refuse.

'OK.'

I finish my cognac. Pick up the blue case full of documents. I leave the little chap with a pleasant smile. Out into the warm sunshine.

Generous bachelors are one of the wonders of the world, as Mother said.

2

I stroll down the tarmac slopes of the Thingholt district.

In fact, I'm late for another meeting here in the old part of the city. That's with Máki. He's the old newshound, sixty-ish, who runs the *News Blog*.

All the same, I'm in no hurry. I'd like to let the wine and lunch settle. I don't make a habit of fine dining during the day.

Máki has a genius for pissing off apparatchiks by exposing both the new and the old secrets of the ruling class. He's one of the few journalists with the patience to dig deep into the hidden sins of the system.

The newshound is waiting at Café Paris. That's a stone's throw from the centre of political power in Iceland.

He's sitting by the window that faces the Parliament building. Table 36. We're regulars here.

Máki's engrossed in a silver laptop. He takes occasional sips of his latte.

He's wearing a shabby old leather jacket. It's an antique that should by rights be in the Árbær museum, just like all the other clothing from centuries gone by.

His wild, mousy hair has grown pretty long again. That could be by choice, or simply because he forgets to get it cut.

I join him with a coffee. Ink-black espresso for me.

Máki has always been bony and lanky. It's as if he forgets to take on board nourishment other than coffee or a double Moscow Mule. Now he's grey and drawn, like he hasn't slept for days.

But his eyes are sharp and you can't miss the concentration on his face.

'I'm getting no end of threats,' he says abruptly.

'What sort of threats?'

'So far today two lawyers have threatened to do their worst. One says he's going to the police and the other one's threatening a libel suit.'

'What have you been writing about now?'

Máki hammers for a moment at the keyboard. Then he turns the screen to face me. The headline screams off the *News Blog* page:

Icelandic Minister was Spy

I skim through the article. I notice right away that the source quoted is anonymous.

The former minister the article is all about is not mentioned by name. But the article states that the man had spied for a foreign intelligence service during his university years at the end of the sixties – and continued to do so after being elected to Parliament and subsequently as a minister.

'Why don't you name the minister?'

'That can wait until the time's right,' Máki replies. 'These last few months I've been working on a book about espionage in Iceland during the Cold War, and this is a taster to warm things up and attract attention. It'll be a bestseller, that's for sure.'

'You don't name your source, or sources.'

'Nope.'

'Reliable?'

'I trust him completely.'

'Him?'

'This is a man who was in the inner circle behind the scenes for decades, all the way back to 1967 when he was at university,' Máki says. 'He's even described how a secret department of the Icelandic police carried out widespread espionage right here. They had sleepers in all of the left-wing movements throughout the sixties, seventies and eighties. He was one of these himself, and now wants to expose the whole thing. It's a hell of a story.'

'He has documents that support his allegations?'

'Some of what he's told me is recollections of his own experience, so those are his narrative,' Máki replies. 'But the minister scoop is connected to a report my source showed me about the US Presidential visit in 1973. Tricky Dicky Nixon and Henry Kissinger came to Reykjavík to meet the President of France. The report states that shortly before the visit, an Icelandic well-wisher provided important information about politicians and dissidents. It's obvious that this man was valued as an informer or a spy. I got a copy of the report and it's stashed away, hoarded like hidden gold.'

'Is the spy named in the report?'

'Yes.'

'OK.'

My coffee is rapidly turning cold.

'It's not stated outright in the article who this minister was spying for,' I add. 'Although the links have to be with the Americans, going by the context.'

Máki grins.

'That's coming. This is just the taster. It's all planned out.'

'The lawyer who threatened a libel action, does he work for this former minister?'

The newshound laughs.

'That's what I thought at first, and then it turned out that his client was once in Parliament for the same party as the minister and is a personal friend of his. The lawyer wasn't amused when I asked if his client too had spied for foreign intelligence services.'

'And the other threat? To take it to the cops?'

'I still don't know whose interests that lawyer has in mind, but he said that it was clear that I'd obtained secret official documents in an illegal manner. He thinks I've stolen official paperwork, and that's absolutely not the case.'

'And your source? Did he steal the document you refer to in the article?'

'I've taken great care to not ask how this material came into his hands. I reckon it's best to not know.'

'You're confident he'll back you up if things get nasty?'

'Yep, sure. He's named in the book.'

'Legally, that gives you a stronger case,' I say. 'How far have you got with the exposé?'

'My source is reading through the text.'

'So the book's written?'

'Yes, pretty much. All that's left is to tighten up the text and get a few more pictures.'

Máki closes his laptop.

'I'm determined to keep going, despite the threats,' he continues. 'Can I point these lawyers towards you if they get on my case again?'

'No problem.'

'Excellent.'

I gaze searchingly at the old newshound.

'It looks to me like you've yet again jumped right into the political elite's secret machinations,' I add. 'The establishment's going to be working overtime behind the scenes for ways to make mincemeat of you. Take care of your sources and documents.'

'Don't you worry,' he says. 'I can look after myself.'

'All the same, take care.'

Máki grins.

'All right, all right. I'll be super-cautious. Just for you.'

3

Thursday 3rd June 2010

Sheesh!

I lean cautiously back in the boss chair, and raise both hands high in the air a couple of times. Time to stretch stiff muscles after a long spell in front of the computer.

It's painful and sweet at the same time.

I long for a massage. Strong, demanding hands. And delectable firewater.

But right now, neither are on offer.

I've spent most of the day going painstakingly through the contents of the dark blue document case.

The Scotsman's minions have worked systematically. They've copied every document that relates to the search for Julia MacKenzie in the summer of 2001. That includes a map of the northern and western parts of the country with information about the search areas covered by the rescue teams.

They've even printed out photographs of the search in progress. There are also photographs Julia sent to her mother in Scotland during her travels. All this information is stored in digital format on a memory stick.

Julia arrived in Seyðisfjörður on Faroese car ferry *Norræna* on Thursday 5th July 2001. She spent the first night in Egilsstaðir, and left there the next morning on her motorcycle, heading for the north of the country.

The next three nights Julia used the hotel at Reykjahlíð as a base. She explored Mývatn, and visited Dimmuborgir, Ásbyrgi and Dettifoss.

On Tuesday 10th she set off for the Highlands for a trip that appears to have lasted nine days, going by her bank card usage, as she paid for an overnight stay at a place deep in Eyjafjörður on the morning of 20th July. That was after the highland trip.

It goes without saying that Julia could have returned to civilisation earlier and paid for accommodation in cash. But there are no indications or clues to that effect in the documents.

On the morning of Sunday 22nd July Julia paid her bill at the Edda Hotel in Akureyri. She had stayed there for two nights.

That same Sunday afternoon she bought fuel in Sauðárkrókur.

After that she vanished without trace.

The police were never able to establish where Julia went from the filling station.

It didn't help that nobody started to look into her movements until twenty-eight days after her disappearance.

The reason was simple.

Nobody realised she had disappeared until she failed to show up for her mother's fiftieth birthday celebration that was held at the family residence in Thorntonhall on 12th August.

She had promised her mother that she would be back in Scotland in plenty of time. She had a ticket booked with *Norræna* from Seyðisfjörður on Thursday 2nd August.

But Julia never arrived at the ferry port in the east of Iceland.

When her mother's repeated phone calls went unanswered the day before the birthday party, and on the day itself, the family contacted police in Edinburgh. They came to the conclusion that Julia had failed to return to Scotland after the trip to Iceland – and they contacted their opposite numbers, Reykjavík's finest.

The search commenced on 19th August, a week after her mother's birthday.

But by then the trail had gone stone cold.

Despite searching for some days across the north and west of the country, the police found no sign of Julia or her motorcycle. No witness came forward to say they had seen or heard from her after her call at that filling station in Sauðárkrókur.

On the other hand, Julia's movements up to 22nd July were adequately recorded and documented, as she paid by bank card for accommodation, food, fuel and fares. After the appeal for sightings of her, several people came forward to say they recalled seeing her. Among these was one of the staff at the Ásbyrgi tourist centre and people who'd been travelling up in the Highlands and who spoke to her both at Askja and Lakagígar.

These people's accounts tallied, in saying that Julia was enjoying her trip. She also hadn't been shy about asking staff or other travellers about things that she saw in the wilderness.

She'd sent some pictures of her trip to her mother. These were from Bjarnarflag, Mývatn and on the way into the Highlands. There was also a photo of her paddling in the green waters of Víti, the Askja crater. The last pictures she had sent were taken while she stayed in Akureyri.

The search for Julia lasted only a few days. The search focused first on Sauðárkrókur and the district around the town. From there the rescue teams searched systematically along the main road from Sauðárkrókur all the way to Borgarnes, checking around the roads and asking at filling stations, kiosks and guest houses along the way. A check was also carried out to see if Julia could be identified on CCTV anywhere between Sauðárkrókur and the Hvalfjörður tunnel, with no success.

Shortly after Julia's mother arrived in Iceland in August 2001, she was informed that an organised search for Julia was hopeless, as the boys in black had no reliable indication of whereabouts in Iceland they should search for her.

Those are some cold-hearted guys.

All the same, I have to confess that the conclusion reached by the police and the rescue squads is in a way understandable.

There's no point giving people false hope. And searches cost money.

My suspicion is that Julia's disappearance is and will continue to be one of life's many unsolved mysteries. But the five million krónur are sitting patiently in the armoured safe in my office. And that's cheering me on.

I call Lísa Björk. She's the sweet little doll who runs my office. She just about comes up to my shoulder.

I hand her the memory stick containing all the data.

'I'd like you to load all this onto our system,' I tell her, and give her a handwritten list of eight individuals.

'Five of these people spoke to Julia in the summer of 2001. Here are the names of the three who co-ordinated the investigation into her disappearance and the search. Could you find current whereabouts and phone numbers for them?'

'Of course.'

I naturally have little faith that any of these eight people can tell me anything about Julia so long after the events. But I feel it's my duty to make an attempt.

That afternoon I spend a long time in front of the computer screen, looking at a picture of Julia. This was taken in Edinburgh just as the new century dawned.

She had a long face. Lively eyes. Broad, smiling lips. And beautiful red-brown hair gathered at the nape of her neck.

A sweet young woman, in the prime of life.

No doubt she'd already been planning this journey to this wonderland of the forces of nature when the picture was snapped ten years ago. For her, this had been a trip that promised so much.

So what happened?

Remember, my dear Stella, that the Almighty owes you no answers, as Mother said.

4

Saturday 5th June 2010

That dazzling light!

Film director Rannveig Thorsteinsdóttir pauses a few metres above me. We're on the slopes of the Snæfellsnes ice cap. Our dour guide, Pálmi, pauses as well. There's also Jón Pétur, the red-haired dude who's in charge of filming the whole razzmatazz.

My snowmobile is red and black. It has the same colour scheme as the snow suit Rannveig handed to me before we headed for the glacier in the morning sunshine – and so does the solid safety helmet.

I cut the engine. The bright snow crackles underfoot as my boots leave clear-cut prints in it.

'We'll film here,' Rannveig calls out. 'Over here, Stella.'

I take off the helmet. Shake out my blonde pride and joy before posing beside Rannveig.

Her production company has a deal with the state broadcaster to make a series, taking well-known women up onto Iceland's ice caps. She specialises in documentaries about women, and accolades have been heaped on her.

Still, I can't figure out how she managed to get me to come all the way up here onto the Snæfellsnes ice cap. But she can be so damn persuasive.

'Smart, famous women on Icelandic glaciers, that's the theme,' she said. 'And is there any one smarter or better known than you?'

It goes without saying that there was only one reply to that.

Rannveig is also too seductive to refuse. She has curves and muscles in all the right places. Long, dark hair, and wonderful lips.

She's sweeter than the sweetest cake Hveragerði has to offer.

There was nothing for it but to join in the fun, even though I have zero interest in glaciers. They're so damn cold and uncomfortable.

'Ready!' Jón Pétur calls as he manoeuvres the camera into position.

'Well, Stella. We're here on the perfect white slopes of

Iceland's most famous glacier, the Snæfellsnes ice cap. It's long been seen as a symbol of the exceptional beauty of Iceland's unspoiled nature,' Rannveig says. 'How do you like it?'

'I wouldn't want to live up here, if that's what you're wondering,' I say with a smile. 'The light up here is way too bright for me.'

'And that's why we have dark glasses,' Rannveig continues. 'There's a tale that English seamen who tried to climb up onto the ice cap in the eighteenth century were blinded by the light and got lost on the ice, and the first Icelanders known to have reached the highest point had rags tied over their eyes to protect them from the brightness.'

'The sunglasses of the time?'

'Exactly. They thought they were climbing the country's highest peak. But the Snæfellsnes ice cap is only 1,446 metres above sea level, so it's not as lofty as many other mountains in Iceland, including Hvannadalshnjúkur, which is the highest.'

'This one's quite big enough for me.'

'For as long as people have lived in Iceland, there has been something magical and otherworldly about the ice cap, especially after Bárður Snæfellsás went into the glacier and made his home there, setting himself up as the lord and protector of both the glacier and the lands around it. If Bárður's story, written seven hundred years ago, is anything to go by, he also hid gold and valuables in a secret place up here, but that treasure has never been found.'

'Shall we look for it? I'm always ready to add to the Stella fund!'

'Unfortunately, I have the feeling that to find Bárður's treasure we would need the magical skills of a real sorcerer.'

Rannveig smiles for the camera.

'That'll do nicely,' she says. 'We'll take the next sequence at the top.'

The ice of the glacier is constantly changing. In some places it's smooth and perfectly white. Elsewhere it's coarse, patchy and uneven.

This time we park the snowmobiles not far below the cold crags that rise high out of the ice. Their surfaces are covered with snow and hung with ice formations that in some places have formed themselves into beautiful sculptures and glittering works of natural art.

Rannveig takes her position in front of the rock face, calls me over and prepares herself to again speak to the camera, and to me.

'The rock formation behind us is known as Miðthúfa,' she says. 'Beyond these three outcrops lies the crater of the volcano that's under the ice cap; this is where the *Journey to the Centre of the Earth* began, described so brilliantly by French novelist Jules Verne more than a hundred and fifty years ago,' she says.

'I saw the film on TV. The one with the Icelandic girl.'

'The view from the top of the ice cap is just fabulous,' she continues, spreading her arms wide. 'We see the magnificent mountains that lie to the east along the Snæfellsnes peninsula, distant highland peaks, the still blue waters of Faxaflói, the Reykjanes lava fields and even as far as Hellisheiði where plumes of steam reach skywards, the innumerable islands and islets of Breiðafjörður, and even all the way to the Westfjords, which are unfortunately hidden by clouds right now.'

I've had enough of the cold, ice and the view.

'What's next?' I ask impatiently when Jón Pétur has finished recording his sequence.

'Now we climb Miðthúfa, you and me,' Rannveig replies.

'Up that steep bastard rock?'

'That's it. I'll go first,' Rannveig says.

She sets off up the snow-caked rock face with a hefty ice axe in her right hand. Jón Pétur records every step she takes up the face of the outcrop, until she's finally standing in triumph on the peak.

She lets a trusty-looking rope fall to me.

Pálmi fixes glittering steel crampons to my boots.

'There you are,' he grunts. 'Off you go.'

I grasp the rope and set off, clambering up in Rannveig's direction. I'm spurred on by the knowledge that Jón Pétur's lens follows my every movement.

'Isn't it fantastic?' Rannveig crows once I'm finally at her side. 'Doesn't looking out from the roof of the world remind you of heaven?'

'If that's heaven, then I don't want to go there,' I reply. But I can't help admiring the wonders nature has to show.

With the help of the rope, half an hour later I slither down from Miðthúfa.

'That went pretty well,' Rannveig says.

But the weather gods hate it when things don't change.

There's a thick fog and banks of cloud gathering fast along

the ice cap. It's the work of a few moments for the cloud to settle on the highest outcrop and almost completely obscure it.

'Shouldn't we make the most of this fog?' Jón Pétur asks.

Rannveig glances at Jón Pétur with interest.

'What are you thinking?'

'How about a sequence with Stella coming out of the fog on a snowmobile?'

'Great idea.'

'No,' Pálmi says, looking grave. 'Not a good idea to be travelling fast up here in fog.'

'But it's such a cool image, man.'

'There are dangerous fissures hidden under what can look like a solid ice surface,' the guide says, fixing Rannveig with a concerned look. 'I'd urge you to be very cautious in the fog.'

Rannveig gives Pálmi an encouraging smile, stuffs her crampons into her backpack, clips her helmet onto her head and starts her snowmobile.

'Well, Stella,' she says. 'Ready to put your foot down?'

I can't refuse that kind of challenge.

We drive slowly along the ice cap towards the edge of the fog bank.

'Go into the fog and then back at full speed,' Jón Pétur yells.

Rannveig vanishes into the dark fog.

I don't hesitate and give it full throttle.

The snowmobile jerks and gathers speed into the silver-grey mist. I hunker down to shelter behind the plastic windshield. I wait to shoot out of the fog again.

But the snowmobile suddenly slews.

The front lifts high. It claws at the air for a long moment. Then it slips backwards into a fissure in the ice cap's white surface, with a terrible grinding and crashing.

I hold on as tight as I can to the handlebars while the snowmobile crashes between white walls.

I lose my grip.

I'm in free-fall into the darkness.

Until I receive a blow to the head and everything turns black.

5

I come round gradually, like emerging from deep sleep. My whole body hurts like hell. Feet. Back. Head.

I'm enveloped in darkness, and damp, and cold.

I'm really very cold.

The questions start to pile up in my mind. They're demanding answers from a brain that's still too confused to think straight.

What happened? Where the hell am I?

I suddenly realise. Anger takes over.

'Fucking, fucking hell!' I yell into the darkness.

All the same, this isn't darkness that frightens me. It's not like it was in the old days when Dad locked me in that windowless cellar and switched off the lights.

No. Not frightened. Just angry.

Proper fucking angry.

But mostly with myself, for having been so stupid as to land in this ridiculous situation.

Anger's good. It provides an opportunity to think clearly, to shake the cobwebs off the thought processes, talk to myself.

I try to figure out my surroundings.

My eyes are adjusting to the gloom. It turns out it's not as totally dark as it seemed when I first regained consciousness.

I'm lying on my side, huddled in a foetal position, as if I've been thrown back in time by that knock-out blow to the head. Emotionally, that is. I cautiously try to roll onto my back, until I'm looking straight upwards.

From a grey-white oval opening far, far above, faint sunlight feels its way down along the rough ice sides of the fissure.

I seem to have landed in an ice cave.

This ice shelf is less than a metre at its widest point and not more than two metres long.

If it hadn't been for this, I'd undoubtedly have plunged much further into the depths.

I feel dizzy, and instinctively roll onto my side again. I retch so hard that sweat breaks out on my forehead.

Below this shelf lies a fearful blackness, a depth of darkness and death. Although I have no idea how deep into the ice cap this fissure extends.

I roll again onto my back. I feel my heart hammer in my chest, like a burst of terrified birdsong.

New questions start to make themselves felt.

Any broken bones? Serious injuries?

I run my right hand over the coarse ice wall.

My shoulder hurts, but I can move all my fingers.

I lift my left hand. That's not broken. That's good.

I try my right leg, and then the left. I try knees and ankles.

There's a searing pain in my left knee. With any luck that's a sprain, not a fracture.

I sit up, slowly and cautiously. I hug the ice wall of the fissure, and massage my knee with gloved fingers.

After a while I look up and stare at the opening the snowmobile tumbled through.

How far did I fall down into the ice cap? Twenty metres? No, more. Forty? Fifty?

I give up trying to guess. Instead I try to imagine what's going on up there. I'm as sure as I can be that Rannveig and her guide have called out the rescue team. Is it just a question of time before I'm rescued and lifted onto the surface of the Snæfellsnes glacier?

That's unless I'm overcome by the cold while waiting for rescuers to arrive.

I search for my phone in one of my snowsuit's pockets. Prod the button to bring the screen to life.

No connection.

'Hell!' I shout in fury.

But I can use it to light up my surroundings. In some places the ice walls are pure blue. In other places they're almost black with mud or sand.

I point the beam of light down into the fissure, without being able to see any bottom to it. But I can see the wreck of the snowmobile. It's jammed between the walls not far below where I am.

On its way down it cut deep grooves in both ice walls, and left behind a shard of broken-off ski stuck in the ice. It sticks out from the wall at one end of the ice cave that saved my life.

I straighten out. With one hand I wipe away the sweat that's running down my face. Then I stare at the red stain on the palm of the heavy glove.

Blood?

Did I receive a head injury during the fall?

I wipe my face again, and look down at my palm.

Yes. Blood.

Fucking hell!

Should I take the helmet off? Check the injury?

Hell, no. Better to wait for help to arrive.

I look again upwards. What's that?

An indistinct shadow flickers across the light from the opening. It's a shape that rocks from side to side, like the pendulum of an old clock.

Is that a rescue line?

I instantly have hopes that help is on the way. But they're dashed immediately.

The line doesn't reach all the way. Nowhere near. Barely halfway.

I see that there's a camera lashed to the end of it.

They must be trying to find out if I'm alive down here in the fissure.

I switch on the phone's flashlight. I wave it at the camera that's probably a good twenty metres above me. I keep waving until it's hauled back to the surface.

Now they should be aware that I'm alive down here in this cold hell.

What wouldn't I give now for a slug of Jack Daniels, my beloved Tennessee nectar? It makes life bearable even at its lowest ebb.

I'm terribly thirsty down here in the cold. There's nothing to drink, except the dirty glacier ice that would no doubt melt in the mouth.

Now I'll just have to stick it out.

As long as we persevere, then death's not here, as Mother said.

6

Survival in a dark ice cave is all about withstanding the cold. Just one lousy hour at a time.

That's why I mustn't lie still. Keep moving, try to keep warm.

But I'm still careful. It wouldn't be difficult to roll off this ice shelf into the depths of this frozen purgatory.

I twist around, lift myself onto my knees.

It hurts like hell.

I decide against trying to stand up. This hole is so damn narrow. But I clap my hands together and raise my hands repeatedly above my head. Anything to keep the blood flowing, fighting off the chill of death.

I use the phone's torch to look around. I look more closely at the ski that broke off the snowmobile as it tumbled, leaving it jutting from the ice wall.

I work my way over to it, and try to free it from the ice.

Finally, I work it free.

OK, that was worthwhile exercise.

The effort helped me forget the cold and the ice cap's desolation.

But the broken ski is of no use to me.

I cast it aside, then hold the phone up to the hole it left in the ice.

What's in there?

There's something that glitters, no doubt about it.

I peer into the hole in the ice wall.

There's something shiny in there.

It's hardly going to be the treasure old Bárður Snæfellsás hid!

I stretch back to take hold of the broken ski. Using the jagged end, I chip away at the ice to make the hole bigger.

After a good while I put it aside and sweep the ice debris away by hand. I hold the light again up to the hole.

The light clearly picks out a heavy ring. It's a ring set with a square red stone. It's a ring that's still on someone's finger.

Hell!

My hand in its cold glove goes instinctively to my mouth. I can hardly believe this.

But there's no doubt about it.

It's a deep-frozen human hand.

I can make out three, four fingers deep in the hole.

Sitting tight to the ice wall, I stretch out my legs. I gaze at the distant brightness of the sky through the opening in the ice cap high above.

Keep calm… Stay calm…

But I can't stop my heart from hammering.

What's worse than sitting completely helpless next to a frozen corpse? It has to be the body of someone who fell into this crevasse in the Snæfellsnes glacier many years ago, and was never found. This is most likely someone who froze to a lonely death.

Is that what's coming to me as well?

A shudder of horror ripples through my whole body.

I cautiously get to my feet, pressing myself tight against the wall. I beat my hands against my body to keep myself warm.

The darkness of the gloomy fissure is unbearable. Then there's the thirst.

And what's the time?

I check the phone again. It's three hours since I regained consciousness down here in the cold.

Where the hell are my rescuers?

I force myself to think of something other than the frozen corpse at my side, the darkness, the cold and the unearthly crackling sound of the ice.

But mostly my thoughts go to my daughter.

Sóley Árdís Blómkvist is being looked after by my cousin Sissi and his wife, Cora, while I'm messing about up here, pretending to be famous on the Snæfellsnes ice cap.

I close my eyes and can see her in front of me, my four-year-old bundle of joy. I can see her bright blue eyes and long fair hair. Her beautiful smile. She's so clever: drawing, singing and dancing. She's a lot smarter than I was at that age.

But I can't get the cold out of my mind.

It's eating its way into the snowsuit, boots and gloves. It bites my face like a vampire.

'Locked and bolted, all the way!'

I repeat the old song's refrain in my mind. Again and again. Just like I did when I was little and vulnerable, at Klettur.

It's another strategy to shut out the cold, and the thirst.

Finally, at long last, I make out movement high above.

I stare at the rescue squad guy who abseils slowly but surely down between the ice walls. The light on his helmet is like sunlight bringing me my own brightness. But no warmth.

He comes to a halt at the edge of the ice shelf.

'Any broken bones?' he asks.

'Don't think so. Did you bring water?'

He hands me a black plastic bottle.

I can't gulp the contents down quickly enough. For the first time in my life, I feel that plain water is almost as sweet as Jacky D.

The man fixes a red harness over my shoulders and around my waist. He clips a rope to it and tugs.

'Ready?'

'Yes, been ready for a long time.'

'Go ahead,' he says into his walkie-talkie. 'Lift.'

I feel a surge of relief as the lifeline lifts me up from the ice shelf.

But it's slow progress up the fissure. I have to push with my hands and feet to stop myself from smashing into sharp, hard ice ridges.

I don't care. I'm on the way home.

Pálmi reaches out, catches hold of my shoulders and hauls me the last few feet onto the ice cap's surface. He leads me a few steps away from the opening before unclipping the harness.

'You've no idea how lucky you are to get out of the glacier alive,' he scowls.

I nod my head. I snatch hold of Pálmi's arm and lean close.

'There's a dead man down there,' I gabble.

The guide looks at me in disbelief, as if he thinks I'm talking crap, mind gone haywire thanks to the fall.

I tell him about the fingers in the ice, and the ring.

'You're certain it's a human hand?'

'Totally.'

Pálmi calls over the leader of the rescue squad. He's a broad-shouldered lad with eyes as grey as stone. He asks me to repeat my story.

There's no mistaking the disbelief on his face.

'We can't not check this out,' he says drily.

There are tears in Rannveig's eyes.

She helps me out of the rescue harness, then takes me over to the rescue squad's snow truck where a dark-haired woman smiles warmly, unclips my helmet and dresses the injury to my head.

21

'There's a helicopter waiting at the edge of the ice,' Rannveig says. 'They'll take you directly to A&E in Reykjavík to be checked out.'

'Is that really necessary?'

'Absolutely. You had a fall of about forty metres into a crevasse and you were down there in the cold for more than four hours.'

Jón Pétur jumps into the snow truck and starts filming.

'TV news wants pictures of the rescue,' he explains.

'Anything for five minutes of fame, yeah?'

Once the helicopter is in the air, I lie back and close my eyes. Long-awaited rest after a dreadful day.

'You mustn't fall asleep,' the dark-haired girl warns. 'Not until the doctors have checked you out.'

'All right.'

Jón Pétur shows me and Rannveig the footage from the fissure.

'That was a good idea, switching on your phone,' he says.

At first all I can see are the coarse pale green walls on the camera's screen. Then there's the faint glow waving back and forth deep in the gloom. That's the light of the torch in my phone.

'Pálmi was certain you'd been smashed to pieces,' he says.

'I'm not surprised.'

'But Rannveig wouldn't have it,' he continues. 'She kept telling us that you're indestructible!'

Rannveig's infectious laugh finally convinces me that the nightmare of the Snæfellsnes ice cap is over at last.

7

Tuesday 8th June 2010

'My mum has a hole in her head,' Sóley Árdís triumphantly informs the teacher at play school, as if I've achieved some amazing feat.

The media have been just as bad. They demanded interviews with me and Rannveig about the nightmare on the Snæfellsnes ice cap. So I had to recount again and again the awful drop, the cold sojourn down there in the crevasse and the long wait for rescue to arrive.

During the TV interviews I held my daughter in my arms, as if showing everyone that I was no longer alone in the world.

'It's great publicity for both of us,' Rannveig said as the last TV interview ended.

'Your film would have got even better publicity if I'd croaked up there on the ice, wouldn't it?'

Rannveig laughs. Even though I wasn't joking.

I made no mention during the Sunday evening interviews of the dead hand.

I received news of that yesterday, after the rescue squad had made certain that they'd found as much of the corpse as they were going to in that area of the ice cap. It's a man's right arm, frozen solid, torn off at the elbow.

The boys in black aired pictures of the ring during the TV news. They encourage anyone who feels that they might recognise it to get in touch with the police immediately.

It's a heavy gold ring. The stone's bright red and square. Deep inside the stone is something I'd not noticed in the gloom of the fissure. It's a blue-black letter L. Or something that resembles an L.

They're also checking fingerprints against data held both here and overseas. There's no certainty that the hand belonged to an Icelander.

I still have a bandage around my head. My left knee hurts like hell. I'm covered all over in bruises.

But I no longer have the patience to take it easy or rest.

All the same, the trauma is making itself felt. The thought that I could easily have lost my life in that hole in the Snæfellsnes glacier verges on the unbearable.

It goes without saying that I've been in deadly danger before now.

But it feels very different this time. That's because I no longer bear responsibility only for myself, but also for my little one.

At play school I kiss Sóley Árdís on both cheeks. I squeeze her tight against me before I head home in my silver steed.

Lísa Björk has been in sole charge of the office for the last few days. It's on the lower floor of the town house that's been mine since I set up my legal practice.

Máki is slurping coffee at the office.

The old newshound makes fun of my appearance. Then he hands me a copy of a summons.

'As you can see, a certain Rögnvaldur Rögnvaldsson has lodged a formal indictment and made a statement to the police to the effect that I've stolen the report that was quoted on *News Blog*,' Máki says. 'He states that this report had been among his documents and is no longer there.'

'You know this guy?'

'Not personally,' Máki replies. 'He ran a legal practice for decades and I understand that he did what was referred to as special work on behalf of the Ministry of Justice and the police.'

'So why does he keep state documents among his personal files?'

'Good question.'

I know the look on Máki's face.

'You know why,' I snap.

'I suspect that Rögnvaldur was the key person behind the Icelandic government's espionage network during the Cold War,' he replies. 'But, since my source hasn't yet been persuaded to state that specifically, I can't yet say anything publicly about Rögnvaldur's role in all this.'

'You mean the source who passed you the report?'

'Yes.'

'Could he have stolen it from Rögnvaldur?'

'It's possible.'

'How possible?'

'I can tell you that they know each other.'

'Your source knows this Rögnvaldur personally?'

'Yes.'

'I understand. Have the city's finest called you in?'

'Yes. We're meeting them at four on Thursday.'

'And what are you going to tell them?'

'Simply that I have read a report of this nature, but where and how are between me and my source,' Máki replies.

'Are you going to name him?'

'No. It's too early for that. His name appears in the book, of course, but that won't be published until November.'

I make myself an ink-black espresso.

'It looks to me like attack is the best form of defence.'

'How so?'

'A summons like this presents justifiable questions concerning the legitimacy of Rögnvaldur Rögnvaldsson keeping secret documents of this nature among his personal files. Is he still working for the authorities?'

'He hit retirement age years ago.'

'So he's no longer a state employee.'

'All the same, I wouldn't want to hit him too hard,' Máki adds.

'Why not?'

'I have my reasons.'

I look Máki up and down.

'Are you going to tell me what these reasons are?'

'Not at this stage.'

'OK. See you at four on Thursday.'

Lísa Björk smiles from her desk at reception. She never fails to be a sweet little doll. She has dark hair, cut short, large, deep eyes. And a cute little nose.

She manages the office. She does all the everyday crap that I no longer have time to deal with properly. She assists with District Court cases. Divorces and inheritance disputes are what she does well.

The first year she was here it occurred to me sometimes to invite her upstairs for a steamy overnight stay. But I always stopped short. I wouldn't want to lose such a fine employee.

Sex and work can often become a poisonous mix.

She's done a good job tracking down those who managed the search for Julia, and most of the people who met a young British geology student up in the Highlands during the summer of 2001.

'Arnaldur Jóhannesson was the search co-ordinator,' she says. 'He lives in Mosfellsbær and is happy to meet you. Chief Superintendent Róbert Sverrisson represented the National Police Commissioner's office, he's still in the job here in

25

Reykjavík. Alfreð Sveinsson was the chief superintendent in Suaðárkrókur in 2001, he's retired now. He says he's happy to meet you, but he's not likely to be coming to Reykjavík any time soon.'

'I see.'

'As far as witnesses who encountered Julia in the Highlands are concerned, I've tracked down three,' Lísa Björk continues. 'Illugi Játvarðsson and his wife Sigríður Jósefsdóttir travelled to Askja with Julia. They live in Blönduós.'

I nod.

'The third witness is Óttar Einarsson, who's a driver. He lives at Varmahlíð in Skagafjörður. They're all prepared to meet you, but if you want to speak to them face to face you'll have to go up north to meet them.'

'Fair enough,' I reply. 'I'll start with Arnaldur and Róbert, as they're both here in the city. Could you book meetings with both of them for later this week?'

'Of course.'

8

Thursday 10th June 2010

The terror on the ice cap had its hooks in me all night long.

Cold, darkness and the sinister groans of nature swam from the depths of my mind to the surface under cover of sleep. The traumatic memories of that horrific sojourn in the fissure in the ice swamped me completely. I couldn't move. Couldn't even cry for help. I was left totally helpless.

I woke in a cold sweat when the nightmare finally left me sometime towards daybreak. The shower's hot deluge went some way to helping me back to normal. That was before I went to wake my little one.

I didn't get much done that morning, but went to call on Ragnar Jónatansson at midday. That's Fat Raggi who's my friend – sometimes – even though he's a chief superintendent.

He's delighted to see me when I drop by his office at the headquarters of the city's finest – and he's just as delighted that I'd been safely rescued from the cold grip of the Snæfellsnes glacier.

'I could hardly believe my ears when I heard you were up on the ice cap,' he grins, making himself comfortable in his chair. 'I thought you were keener on partying downtown than on the wonders of Iceland's mountains.'

'I've never been up on an ice cap before,' I reply. 'And I won't be doing it again.'

Raggi laughs. He's no mountain goat himself.

It goes without saying that the senior figures among the city's finest are rarely pleased to see me. Most of them make a run for it when they see me coming.

Raggi is the exception that proves the rule. He's a chief superintendent you can speak to in confidence. Sometimes, at any rate.

He hasn't made much progress in gaining control of his waistline. But his scalp is smooth and polished so it gleams. It's a few years since he gave up encouraging hair to grow on his head.

I decided to call on Raggi because of the paucity of information I have about Rögnvaldur Rögnvaldsson, the guy who's taking Máki to court.

But I found an old article in *Morgunblaðið*. So I know that Rögnvaldur was born in the Thingvellir district in 1933. He studied at the Reykjavík Junior College and then the University of Iceland. He ran a legal practice in Seltjarnarnes for decades. He married at twenty and was widowed in 1970. He has one son, Thorsteinn, who runs a company in the Westman Islands.

There's no mention anywhere of Rögnvaldur having worked for years on behalf of the Ministry of Justice or the Reykjavík Commissioner of Police.

Has Máki's source been leading the old newshound up the garden path?

Raggi leans back in his chair, smiles, and occasionally pats his belly. He's sitting beneath the big aerial picture of Bíldudalur, the village where he started his police career. But once I mention Rögnvaldur Rögnvaldsson, his expression turns serious. His sharp eyes focus on me with interest.

'I see,' he says at last. 'You're representing *News Blog*?'

I give him a sweet smile.

'This can hardly be something that comes across your desk?'

'No,' Raggi says. 'But I keep an eye on what goes on.'

'I'd never heard of this Rögnvaldur before,' I say. 'He's an antique of some sort, isn't he? But I understand he worked for you for a long time?'

'For us?'

'Yes. For the Commissioner of Police and for the Minister of Justice.'

'There are plenty of lawyers who have done work for us over the years.'

'Do you know him personally?'

Raggi shifts in his seat.

'I met him a few times in my younger years,' he replies at last.

'So what was his role on your behalf?'

'I'm afraid you're barking up the wrong tree here,' he said drily. 'Those are questions for the Commissioner.'

'Come on.'

'That's the way it is.'

I meet Raggi's calm but steadfast gaze.

'It seems spooky to me if this guy was right at the centre of things here for years on end, without it being mentioned anywhere officially,' I say. 'This isn't some secret fucking service.'

'I feel that the word "if" is the key one in your assertion,' he replies.

'That may well be. So far. But that's going to change.'

'Sure about that?'

'There's nothing that spurs me on more than the establishment putting up walls of silence. You know that.'

Raggi gets to his feet.

'This conversation is over,' he says.

I make for the door without another word. Despite the pain in my knee, I storm along the corridor, down to reception and out into the sunshine.

In reality, Raggi's negative response doesn't take me by surprise. He's a long-serving apparatchik and jobsworth. Although he's a cut above all the rest of them.

It was worth a try.

That conversation convinces me that the city's finest have something to hide when it comes to Rögnvaldur Rögnvaldsson.

For the next few hours I put all my energy into the Stella Fund. I deal with a bunch of stuff in record time. Final demands, legal threats. Hints for my broker on what to buy and sell.

The time passes far too quickly.

Máki's already there to make his statement to the police when I arrive. He's sitting facing two men.

One of them's a lawyer I'm familiar with.

Símon Andrésson.

He's a thoroughly malevolent Ministry of Justice mandarin.

'Good of you to show up,' Haraldur Haraldsson sneers. He's a renowned misogynist and we're crossed swords before.

I glance at my gold watch. It's a beautiful gift from Ludmilla. A few years ago she was my passion.

It's one minute past four.

'Is your time cock-eyed?' I ask impudently.

Máki can't keep a smirk off his face.

'Why's there another lawyer present?'

'I invited Símon to join the meeting as an expert adviser,' Haraldur says without further explanation.

'Expert in what?'

Haraldur doesn't reply. Instead he embarks on a formal presentation of Rögnvaldur Rögnvaldsson's summons which relates to assertions published by Máki on *News Blog*.

'Your article quotes a report that has been stored for years among Rögnvaldur's personal files and which has now disappeared, without his consent,' he says. 'By publishing this you have quoted publicly an official document, which you have either stolen or you got some accomplice to steal.'

The men get straight to work. They demand that Máki hand over his source for the article so that they can establish whether or not this is the document in question.

'I can't hand over anything,' Máki says without missing a beat. 'For the simple reason that I have no such document in my possession.'

'Are we therefore to believe that the assertion in your article is baseless?' Haraldur asks.

'No. Of course not.'

'You have seen this report?'

This is where I interrupt.

'You refer repeatedly to "this report" as if there is documented evidence that the report Rögnvaldur mentions is in existence. Has he provided any evidence to support this?'

Símon clears his throat.

'It is beyond doubt that this report exists and has been in Rögnvaldur Rögnvaldsson's keeping,' he says.

'Beyond doubt? Do you seriously expect my client to take such an assertion at face value without any supporting evidence?'

'Written confirmation will be made available at a later stage of this case, if necessary,' the lawyer replies.

Haraldur glares at Máki.

'Answer the question,' he says.

'What was the question again?'

'Have you seen the report that you quote in your article?'

'I quoted in *News Blog* a document to support the assertions that were made. Of course that means I read the report.'

'From whom did you get this document?'

'From a source.'

'Who?'

'As a journalist I am naturally bound to keep my sources confidential.'

'You're refusing to identify the person who showed you the document?'

'I am neither able nor willing to betray my source without that person's written agreement.'

'Are you prepared to request such an agreement?' Símon asks.

'It's not something I've considered,' Máki answers. 'On the

other hand, it's no secret that some of my sources make a habit of identifying themselves after a few months.'

'In what sense?'

'That's in connection with a book I'm working on.'

'Book?' the lawyer parrots. 'You're writing a book about this same subject matter?'

'Yes,' Máki replies with a smile. 'I'm working on a book about espionage in Iceland during the Cold War.'

'And your source will be named in this book?'

'Yes.'

It hadn't occurred to me that Máki would brag here and now about his book. Otherwise I'd have headed him off.

Haraldur and Símon exchange glances, as if they're sharing the same thought. I try to lead them in another direction.

'There's an aspect of this that I don't understand,' I say. 'At what point in the official system does a senior citizen have a licence to store secret documents relating to domestic or foreign government business in their own home?'

Neither of the pair look likely to provide an answer to this question.

'Unless Rögnvaldur also purloined this report? Took it home from working for you, back in the day?'

There's a deathly silence in response.

'We're all aware that Rögnvaldur worked for you for decades? The Commissioner of Police and the Ministry of Justice. That's correct, isn't it?'

Haraldur breaks the silence.

'I don't understand what you're driving at,' he says coldly, and turns to Máki. 'Where is this report now?'

'I've no idea,' the newshound replies right away. It's as if there's nothing more normal than lying to the cops.

'Did you make a copy?'

'No.'

'The source who showed you the document, who is this?'

'I've already answered that question. That remains confidential.'

Now the evil lawyer puts his oar in again.

'Would you be prepared, today or this evening, to find out if your source is prepared to identify himself, for the purposes of this investigation?' Símon asks.

'It doesn't cost anything to ask,' Máki replies. 'But I imagine he'll prefer to wait until the book is published.'

'I would urge you to make a request at the earliest opportunity.'

Máki sends me an enquiring glance.

'My client is prepared to explore the possibility, although that in no way alters his fundamental obligation to protect his source under all circumstances.'

'Let's hope it doesn't come to that,' Símon says quietly.

I look into the man's eyes. I see nothing there but cold determination.

This is one spooky guy.

I've a strong intuition that Máki would have done better to keep his mouth shut.

9

Friday 11th June 2010

Arnaldur Jóhannesson, who co-ordinated the search for Julia, is a robust man in his fifties; fair hair, barrel chest. He has a weather-beaten face that indicates that being outdoors in all weathers is what he lives and breathes.

He lives in an old black-painted, timber-framed house on Reykjavegur, up in the popular bucolic paradise of Mosfellsbær. He's hard at work in his garden as my Merc rolls to a halt outside.

He puts his garden tools aside, and wipes away the sweat from his forehead with the back of his hand. He offers me a seat at an ancient wooden garden table.

'Hang on,' he says, like a man used to issuing instructions. He disappears inside the house. When he comes back with two cans of beer, he hands one to me. He pops the tab on his and glugs cold beer.

I don't like beer. It's so damn fattening. And it tastes like crap.

On top of that, the only alcohol I prefer is the Tennessee nectar. Or a decent wine with a succulent meal.

I put the can to one side without opening it.

Then I check the man out for a moment.

'My secretary told you what this is about, didn't she?'

Arnaldur nods.

'It's ten years since the search for this foreign girl,' he says. 'Why's this coming up again now?'

'Julia MacKenzie's mother still hopes to find out what became of her.'

'I understand, naturally. Events like this one are always tough for the relatives, but surely nothing relating to her disappearance has changed?'

'Only that I'm going over all of the case documentation. Looking for that elusive needle in a haystack, or something like that.'

'Those of us who were involved in the search were in a hopeless position right from the start,' Arnaldur says. 'On the day she disappeared, nobody knew where she was heading. The only confirmed sighting we had was that she had filled up her bike's tank at the filling station in Sauðárkrókur. The best guess we had was that she was heading towards Reykjavík and intended to then take the south coast route to Seyðisfjörður, where she had a crossing with *Norræna* booked about two weeks later. But we had nothing conclusive to work on. This was just a guess that we worked on as a basis, and which yielded no results. If you've been through all the files for the search and the investigation, then you've no doubt seen for yourself how hopeless it was.'

'There's one thing that caught my eye reading through the files.'

Arnaldur leans forward. He stares.

'What's that?'

'What all the documentation has in common is an assumption that Julia had an accident of some kind.'

'Yes, the search was carried out on that basis.'

'But considering where and how she vanished, and that no sign of her bike or belongings were found, there's another explanation that seems to me more likely.'

'Which is?'

Arnaldur straightens out. He raises the beer can to his lips and takes a swig.

'Yes. It seems to me to be strange that Julia's disappearance was not investigated as a potential kidnapping or murder.'

'I see what you mean,' Arnaldur says. 'But it wasn't my evaluation. The police handled that. I just co-ordinated the search itself.'

'But you must have formed an opinion of what could have happened to Julia?'

'When searching for people, I work solely with the facts as they are presented. The police never discussed the possibility that this could have been a crime. It wasn't ever part of the picture, as far as I recall.'

'How come?'

'You'll have to ask the police about that.'

'Do you have an opinion on this now? With the benefit of hindsight?'

'There have certainly been disappearances in Iceland that could be deliberate,' Arnaldur replies. 'But it's one thing to have a suspicion, and another to come across evidence that there's some basis for that kind of suspicion. As far as I'm aware, there was no information at the time that indicated she could have been the victim of an assault, and I don't know of anything since that points in that direction.'

But Chief Superintendent Róbert Sverrisson, who oversaw the investigation into Julia's disappearance, ought to know.

As I park the silver steed outside his house in Gravarvogur, he's carrying stuff out into the family caravan. Clearly, they're off on their travels.

'Leaving this evening,' he says.

Róbert is in his sixties, tall and skinny.

I clamber up into the caravan behind him. There's a sort of sofa to sit on.

'We did everything we could for this girl's family,' he says in his hoarse smoker's voice. 'If you have the police reports, then you'll see that we did everything possible to reach a conclusion. We simply found no solid indications of what might have happened to her, neither in interviews with witnesses, nor with a detailed examination of the digital trail.'

'Isn't it likely she could have fallen into the hands of a criminal?'

The chief superintendent shakes his head.

'There's nothing to indicate that,' he replies. 'She didn't have any altercations with anyone on her travels. Quite the opposite, as witnesses said that she got on well with everyone she encountered in the Highlands.'

'Yes, they say she was open and friendly. But was she maybe too friendly with the wrong person?'

'Nobody we spoke to gave us the slightest suspicion of anything like that. We had no reason to suspect that the girl had been the victim of an assault.'

'When people disappear with no explanation, like Julia, and aren't found, despite a search, isn't there good reason to suspect a crime?'

'People have vanished in Iceland before and never been found, without any indication of foul play,' Róbert replies. 'There need to be positive indicators for that to happen, and in this case we had none at all.'

'You still think that Julia lost her life in an accident in some unknown location?'

'Yes,' Róbert says. 'I have to admit I find it odd that after all these years no traveller has stumbled across a body or the motorcycle, but that could be because she went somewhere remote, or she and the bike could have ended up in the sea or a lake. As long as there's no new evidence to the contrary, that still seems to me to be the most likely explanation.'

I've made no progress in looking into Julia's disappearance as I hurtle in the silver steed down Ártúnsbrekka on the way home to my red town house.

Máki calls my mobile.

'Now the sparks are starting to fly,' he says.

'How so?'

'They're getting at me in the media,' Máki replies. 'There are interviews online, two politicians and a historian, all giving an opinion that my assertions about an Icelandic spy are fabrications from top to bottom.'

'Don't tell me you're surprised they're trying to discredit you?'

'No, certainly not. I just see it as great publicity for the book.'

'Are you going to respond?'

'Yes, but only on *News Blog*. Just finishing a new article.'

'Have you spoken to your source?'

'I called him last night,' Máki says. 'He always expected a media furore around the book's publication, so these interviews won't take him by surprise. But the summons is another matter. It had never occurred to him that Rögnvaldur would accuse us of theft. He's going to come into town on Sunday and we'll go over the whole thing and decide what the best strategy is. On the other hand, the summons means the publisher wants his own lawyers to read the manuscript and assess the likelihood of prosecution.'

'Is that a problem for you?'

'I couldn't say, not this far ahead.'

'Is this publisher likely to be frightened by establishment threats?'

'Not that I've ever noticed up to now. But who knows? The tentacles of power stretch under the surface in every direction.'

'You're sticking to your guns?'

'Yes, of course,' Máki replies.

No change there in the old warrior. He sees giving an inch as betrayal.

But that's not always right. Sometimes you can snooker an opponent by taking an alternative route to an objective.

Never swerve when the road ahead is straight, as Mother said.

10

Saturday 12th June 2010

My silver steed is carrying me up to the north.

Once the Hvalfjörður tunnel is behind me I put Sinéad on the stereo. This is music to get horny to, and it flows through me. That's while I digest that morning's news of the city's finest and their investigation into the hand I found in the ice.

They've checked fingerprints against their own records. There's no match. That doesn't mean that hand belongs to a foreigner. It just means it's someone who never found his way onto the police database.

'Interpol is checking for matching fingerprints on databases in Europe and North America,' a spokesman for the boys in black said on the radio.

There's cloud cover over Holtavörðuheiði and it's a chilly day. Even though it's the middle of June, it's not exactly summery. There are still remains of snowdrifts here and there, especially in the gullies up on top of the heath.

The media have been buzzing around the ring on the frozen hand for the last few days. Not just the local news. The discovery has attracted interest from online news outlets overseas.

The story is the *Ring of Death* found beneath an Icelandic glacier.

The hook is the blue-black letter that can be seen deep in the ring's stone, or under it. Someone came up with the theory that the ring has to be a symbol of a secret society. But nobody has come forward claiming to have seen a similar ring before.

All the while, Sinead croons of the sweet pleasures of the night. I'm up for that, should the opportunity present itself.

Sigríður Jósefsdóttir and Illugi Játvarðsson live in a detached house overlooking the river. Blandá flows fast through Blönduós on its way to the sea.

This is a couple in their thirties. They look young and healthy, and they're both teachers. There's coffee and doughnuts in their living room.

'You can see the girl in four of the pictures we took on that trip,' Sigríður says, handing me a thick photo album. She's marked the photos of Julia Mackenzie with yellow Post-its.

'You travelled together for three days, didn't you?'

'That's right,' Illugi confirms. 'It's not as easy as you might think to get all the way to Askja on a motorbike. We met Julia at Jökulsá á Fjöllum. She spoke to us and said that she was having trouble crossing the river. We had our big pickup, so we offered to ferry her and the bike across. It turned out that we were all going in the same direction so she stayed with us all the way to the Askja lake. After that our ways parted.'

'How come?'

'We were heading southwards towards Sprengisandur. Julia intended to go and take a look at Kverkfjöll and then travel down to see the Tungnafell glacier, and from there go northwards to Eyjafjörður. She had everything carefully planned in advance.'

I examine the pictures for a while.

'How did she come across to you?'

'She knew what she was doing and was well organised,' Sigríður replies. 'I could tell right away that she had planned her trip with care. She was well equipped and had read up on all the places she wanted to see on the way. I didn't see her as likely to have an accident or get lost in the Highlands. Not at all.'

'Julia sent her mother a picture of herself in the water at Víti. Did one of you take that photo?'

They exchange enquiring glances.

'There's no possibility that she could have taken that picture herself,' I add.

'I don't recall taking a picture of her there,' Illugi says.

Sigríður shakes her head.

'Did she meet anyone other than you during that time?'

'We weren't keeping tabs on her, but I noticed that she spoke to a lot of people,' Sigríður says. 'She was very personable and struck up acquaintance easily.'

'The first picture was taken crossing Jökulsá á Fjöllum,' Illugi says. 'In this one we're at Herðubreið and the other two are from Askja.'

In the fourth and final picture, Julia is tinkering with the motorcycle.

A dark-haired, middle-aged man is standing on the other side of the bike and appears to be having a conversation with her.

'Who's that?' I ask.

They peer at the picture.

'He's not someone I know,' Illugi eventually replies.

'I've a feeling that he was a driver or a guide who was there with a group,' Sigríður says. 'But I can't be sure.'

'Could I hold on to this picture?'

'That's fine with us,' Illugi says.

I put the photo in my russet-brown briefcase, and thank them for their time. Then I head towards Skagafjörður.

On the way I take care to keep the silver steed at a reasonable speed. I don't care to be caught out over the speed limit in a part of the country where the cops are notorious for ambushing motorists to rack up fines that flow into the government's coffers.

Óttar Einarsson is washing the dust from a pale-coloured minibus when I turn up. This is outside the filling station in Varmahlíð, right next to the main road.

He's a chubby guy, looks to be in his fifties. He wears a black baseball cap.

He takes me into the café next to the petrol pumps, and orders himself a burger and a glass of pop.

I don't have any appetite.

'Yes, I met this girl up in the Kverkur mountains,' he says.

'How did that come about?'

'She came and chatted to us about all sorts.'

'Us?'

'I had a group of twelve in the bus, all foreigners. We stayed at the hostel there, and so did the girl.'

'Going by the guest book, she stayed two nights.'

'That may well be, but our group was there for just one night. I remember clearly that she talked to some of the foreigners. She asked a lot of questions about the ice caves up there and wanted to hear about people's travels around the region in the old days.'

I show Óttar the photo of Julia and the motorcycle.

'Do you know who that is in the picture with her?'

Óttar holds the picture away from his face, as if he's long-sighted.

'Isn't that Geiri Sveins?'

'Who's that?'

'He runs the stables at Gullinhamrar and he takes groups up into the Highlands on horseback in the summer. All the horsey people know Geiri Sveins.'

Geiri from Gullinhamrar?

There's no police statement from him.

That's for sure.

So I've found one new witness who met Julia in the Highlands.

'Where's his place?' I ask Óttar.

'Gullinhamrar is in the Skagi district, north of Sauðárkrókur.'

I decide to catch up with the horse guy before I head back south. Even though there's no certainty he knows anything about Julia.

But you have to take what little you can when the pickings are slim.

11

Aaah!

I stand stock still under the rush of water. The sweet feeling of wellbeing rushes through me and smoothly recedes.

I finally turn off the shower, and dry the moisture from my long, fair hair. My delight. In front of the mirror in the little bathroom, I dry myself carefully.

The injury to my head is now barely visible.

I make my way slowly to the bedroom. Pull the bedcover off the duvet, and stack the pillows up against the headboard. I sit naked in bed. Here I examine the bruises that fade a little more every day. Just like the memory of the sojourn in the crevasse in the glacier.

I've invited Alfreð Sveinsson, who was chief superintendent of the Sauðárkrókur police force in 2001, to meet me in the hotel bar. I'm expecting him in half an hour.

But first I want to google Geiri at Gullinhamrar. He's the witness nobody seems to have spoken to about Julia's disappearance. It doesn't take long to find out that he's been running a stud farm and stables at Gullinhamrar since 1997, along with his brother Jósteinn.

The stables' website shows plenty of pictures of people on horseback here and there in the countryside, including up in the Highlands. There's no shortage of pictures of Geiri with his beloved horses.

It may well be that he knows nothing important. We'll find out.

I don't bother with underwear, but put on a soft, pink blouse. The skirt is white leather, short and clinging. Black boots reach over my knees.

In front of the mirror I touch up my face. Then a drop of Midnight Heat behind each ear and under my chin.

I'm ready for anything tonight.

It goes without saying that I'm not going to these lengths for an old guy drawing a pension.

But any bar always offers a chance of action.

Alfreð looks pretty good for his age. He's on the short side, but muscular, as if he trains with weights. His hair is fair, with no sign of a bald patch.

I order a double Jack Daniels. The old chap asks for whisky, with ice and water. We take seats to one side of the bar.

'I don't see why you've come all the way up north to meet me,' he says. 'I don't know any more about this woman's disappearance than what's already in the police reports from 2001.'

'I've gone very carefully through all of your reports, both the police and the rescue squads,' I tell him. 'What stands out is that Julia's disappearance was never investigated as a kidnapping or a murder. Why was that?'

'You can't treat every disappearance as a crime,' he says with a frown. 'Experience shows clearly that the majority of disappearances are due to accidents of some kind. Working on the assumption that the individual has been in an accident is the standard starting point.'

'And when a search turns up nothing? As was the case here?'

'That means that we didn't identify the accident location.'

'Julia simply vanished. Not just her, but her motorcycle, luggage and all her belongings. Didn't that arouse suspicion that this could have been a crime?'

'What it comes down to is that we had nothing to indicate that a crime had been committed.'

'And what's your feeling now that she's not been found more than a decade on?'

Alfreð empties his glass.

'It's a case I haven't even thought about for years. I'm retired and don't spend my time digging through old investigations,' he says drily. 'I feel it's unfortunate that we weren't able to recover a body. That speaks for itself. But she's far from the only missing person that Iceland's natural world hasn't given back. That's the way it is.'

'Would you rule out someone having kidnapped and murdered Julia?'

'Unless you can present some evidence indicating that was the case. Can you do that?'

I shake my head.

'That's the way it is, unfortunately.'

'Another whisky?'

'I never turn down a good offer,' Alfred replies.

He's well into his second glass when I ask about Geiri at Gullinhamrar.

'What does he have to do with this?'

'He met Julia in the Kverkur hills. But you don't seem to have taken a statement from him. Why's that?'

'We advertised for people who had been aware of the woman's movements and we spoke to everyone who came forward and said they had spoken to her. I don't recall if Geiri was one of those or not.'

'Assuming I have all of the case files, then he wasn't interviewed.'

'How do you know he met this woman?'

'A couple in Blönduós took some pictures of Julia up in the Highlands. One of them shows her in conversation with this Geiri.'

'I imagine it's more than likely she met more people than those who came forward,' the old man says. 'But that doesn't necessarily have any bearing on her disappearance, as she vanished a couple of days after coming down from the Highlands.'

We chat for a while about different angles of the investigation without me learning anything new.

As far as he's concerned, it's case over. Dead and buried.

'I feel it's not right for you to be giving the girl's mother any false hopes of this case ever being resolved,' he says as he gets to his feet. 'If the body's found somewhere at some point, then it'll be purely by chance.'

'I haven't given her any hope of the case being resolved,' I reply sharply. 'Quite the opposite.'

Once Alfreð has gone on his way, I glance around the bar. I see there are more guests now.

Two young guys come and chat to me. They look the right side of forty. They say they're in banking, travelling to Akureyri. They offer me a drink.

I accept, listen to them bragging for a while. But I'm in no mood for arrogant jocks tonight.

I've already spied a sweet chick who's hardly a day over thirty. Petite, short red hair and brown eyes.

She unerringly catches my eye. She looks away a couple of times. But her eyes are always drawn back in my direction.

Finally, she gets to her feet and heads for the ladies.

I follow, glass in hand.

She's fixing her dark red lipstick.

'*Hæ*,' she breathes. There's excitement in her eyes as she looks at me in the mirror.

Her voice is husky with suppressed passion.

I know that look in her eyes.

'Room six,' I say.

She nods.

I finish my drink on the way up the stairs.

She doesn't keep me waiting. She doesn't say a word as I lock the door behind her. But her eyes betray her desire.

I lift her dress over her head, and unclip her bra. That's before I kiss her.

She moans with delight as I drop to my knees and slowly roll her white underwear down her legs.

This night's going to be hot and steamy.

12

Sunday 13th June 2010

We let lust have free rein.

By the time she pulled on her clothes around three, we had both given in totally to the pleasures of the flesh. We emptied every drop from the cup of carnal pleasure.

She disappeared into the night without mentioning her name.

The rocks that give Gullinhamrar its name loom high over the verdant pasture. High up against the cliff face a couple of outbuildings are falling apart.

I come to a halt early in the morning in front of a newish single-storey farmhouse perched not far from the main road. A much older place, a dilapidated concrete house, squats on a grassy hillock a hundred metres away up the slope. Behind it the sunlight glitters on an old cylindrical silage tower.

Two large new buildings stand side by side not far from the newer farmhouse, a stable and a barn. That's where Geiri Sveins is trying to break in a young stallion inside a fenced paddock.

He speaks gently to the stallion, who doesn't take it well.

'Looking for a horse?' he asks as I approach.

'I'm looking for information,' I reply.

He dismounts, tethers the horse to one of the fence posts, strides out of the paddock and shuts the gate, extending a hand with a smile on his face.

He seems a cheerful soul, solidly built, with an outdoors kind of face. His hair's dark and untidy.

'We have horses for all age groups,' he says. 'Everything from prize winners who can go at a gallop, and quiet, reliable horses for children and anyone not accustomed to riding.'

'You were part of a group that rode up to Askja in the summer of 2001, weren't you?'

He scratches his head and stares in surprise.

'I've ridden up to Herðubreiðarlindir and Askja every summer for the last ten years or so,' he says. 'That's one of our regular group outings.'

I open my russet-brown briefcase and pick out the photo of Julia and Geiri.

'You remember this girl?'

Geiri squints at the picture.

'I meet so many people here and there,' he says.

'She's British. Julia MacKenzie.'

'Yes, hold on. I spoke to her up by Askja, didn't I?'

'The picture was taken there.'

'That's right. She was a very switched-on girl, if I recall correctly, very interested in Icelandic horses.'

'So you remember her?'

'Yes, I should say so. I asked her something about her bike, as you don't see so many of those up there at Askja. I even offered her a decent horse to ride instead of the motorbike.'

'And she turned you down?'

''It wasn't a serious offer,' he laughs. 'I remember now that she came with me to take a look at the horses and she got to sit on one. She'd never ridden such a small horse, but had often ridden larger ones in her own country. She was from Edinburgh, wasn't she?'

'She was studying at university there.'

'I recall that I invited her to stop by if she was passing, and she'd have a chance for a proper ride then,' Geiri continues.

'Really?'

'Yep, think so. But I don't remember she ever showed up.'

'You're absolutely sure of that?'

'Yes. I'd certainly have remembered if she'd paid us a visit.'

He seems sincere – and harmless.

A few horses stand by the fence in front of the new building further up.

'You have a lot of horses?'

'I have forty or so, and my brother Jósteinn has about the same,' Geiri replies proudly. 'That includes foals.'

'Are there many people working for you?'

'There's just the yard manager who's here all year round.'

'And in the summer?'

'Then we have a couple of youngsters working here.'

'You take many groups up into the Highlands yourself?'

'I always take the four-week trip in July to Herðubreið and Askja,' Geiri replies. 'Then I take shorter trips as well.'

Four weeks in July?

I give Geiri a questioning look.

'When in July does this long trip to Askja end?'

'I always try to be home before the bank holiday weekend.'

I think for a moment.

'So you'd have been up in the Highlands on the 22nd of July 2001?'

'Yes, I reckon so.'

'If Julia had travelled here to Gullinhamrar that day or the next, who would she have met here?'

'Probably the youngsters, or Alexander.'

'Who's Alexander?'

'Our yard manager. He's always in charge here when I'm away.'

'Where is he?'

Geiri glances around.

'Well, I expect he's up there in the stable.'

'I need a word with him.'

'Not a problem, my dear.'

Geiri pulled a mobile phone from a pocket of his green boiler suit, calls the yard manager and asks him to come on down for a moment.

Alexander is tall and skinny, black-haired and dark-eyed.

Looks to be around forty. He's hellishly good-looking and he knows it.

'This lady's asking about a British girl who might have called on us a few years ago,' Geiri says, scratching his head again.

Alexander's face freezes for a moment.

'A British girl?'

His voice is deep and dark. There's an accent there.

I open my briefcase again. Out comes the photo of Julia.

'Do you recall seeing this woman?' I ask.

Alexander takes the picture.

'No,' he replies almost instantly, and hands it back to me.

His smile is forced, and it doesn't reach his eyes.

'She could have been here on the 22nd of July 2001?'

He shakes his head.

'Don't you want to take a closer look at the picture?'

'No. I've never seen this person.'

For a moment I stare into the man's face. He tries to smile.

'That's it, my dear,' Geiri says.

I hesitate and replace the picture in my briefcase.

'Is that all?' Alexander asks.

'Yes,' I reply shortly. 'For now.'

He turns on his heel. Heads back to the stable.

I look around this peaceful rural scene with a nagging

disquiet in my heart. Not that I have any direct reason for that.

Most likely it's feminine intuition. Or something like that.

I thank Geiri for his time. Then I drive slowly off in the silver steed. Course set for Reykjavík.

It's only as I'm approaching Sauðárkrókur that it occurs to me that neither Geiri nor Alexander asked why I was asking about whether Julia could have called there a decade previously.

Neither of them.

Why this lack of curiosity?

13

Sóley Árdís loves the merry-go-round at the petting zoo.

I give in and let her have her third go of the day on it. She sits stiffly on her brightly-coloured wooden horse and waves.

She's fascinated by animals. She calls out to the seals as they emerge from the water in the pool. She whoops as she runs after the hens. To get the best view she can of the fox, she runs along the fence. She even tries to pat the sulky bull in the cowshed.

After walking back and forth around the petting zoo, she puts away a long-awaited ice cream in the café. I opt for hot coffee and a waffle with jam and cream. Even though it's as fattening as hell. I take the opportunity to switch my phone back on.

Máki has called a few times.

I call back.

'Where are you, woman?' he demands.

'I'm enjoying life with Sóley Árdís,' I reply. 'What's up?'

'You haven't heard the news?'

'What news?'

'What happened at Skálholt last night?'

'No.'

'I can't talk about this on the phone,' he says. 'We have to meet.'

'We'll be home around six.'

'Not earlier?'

'Six-thirty at the latest.'

'See you then.'

It sounds like the old newshound's nerves have finally got the better of him.

Sóley Árdís is engrossed in her ice cream.

I take a look at the news on my phone. Immediately, I see the headline Máki was talking about.

Couple die in Skálholt fire

According to news reports a fire broke out in Thorláksbúð, next to the cathedral at Skálholt. When this controversial building was opened in the morning, black smoke gushed out. The staff at Skálholt were able to extinguish the fire by the time the fire brigade arrived.

The bodies were found lying side by side on the floor. The expectation is that they died of smoke inhalation, although autopsies haven't yet been carried out.

The origin of the blaze is unknown. The names and ages of the deceased aren't given.

A fire. A fatal accident. And Máki on the brink of a nervous breakdown.

What connects all these?

I switch off the phone, so I can enjoy the day with my daughter.

This is our time.

Máki's waiting in his black Skoda as we glide to a halt in the silver steed. He jumps out as soon as he sees us.

He's pale and his face is drawn. It looks like he's had a serious shock.

I show him to the kitchen.

'Get yourself a coffee,' I say, pointing him to the espresso machine.

I take Sóley Árdís into the living room. I switch on the TV and select a children's channel showing cartoons.

'Mum'll be in the kitchen,' I tell her.

I go back to Máki, who's sitting at the table by the window without having switched on the coffee machine.

'Don't you want a coffee?' I ask.

He shrugs.

I make two espressos. Put them on the table. I sit opposite Máki.

'You look like you need something to buck you up.'

Máki takes his cup. He sips, and sips again.

'I'm totally fucked,' he says.

'I saw the news item about the fatalities at Skálholt,' I say. 'Were they close relatives of yours, or what?'

'Much, much worse than that.'

'Let's hear it.'

'I got confirmation around midday today,' he continues. 'The man who was found dead in Thorláksbúð is....was, my source.'

'The one who passed you Rögnvaldur's report?'

'Not just the report,' Máki replies. 'Thorsteinn's account forms the bulk of the narrative. Without him, I'm totally screwed.'

'His name's Thorsteinn?'

'Thorsteinn Rögnvaldsson.'

'Rögnvaldsson?'

Máki nods.

'You've got it right,' he says. 'My source was Rögnvaldur Rögnvaldsson's only son.'

'So the old man was in fact prosecuting his son for theft?'

'If you want to look at it like that. Except that he presumably didn't know that the information had come to me direct from Thorsteinn. But the heart of the matter is that I no longer have access to my source. Thorsteinn was my shield in this fight. Now I'm defenceless and the knives are out for me. This is going to be a real-time crucifixion.'

I stare at Máki.

'You didn't have a written agreement with Thorsteinn concerning the book?'

'Signing an agreement was one of the things we were going to sort out this weekend,' the newshound says. 'Up to now our relationship has been built on trust and confidence.'

'You have nothing from him in writing?'

'Of course I have emails and letters he sent me, and notes we passed between us.'

'Named?'

'Yes. The emails are in his name, and many of the letters are on the Westman Islands company notepaper.'

'That's something,' I say.

'Thorsteinn was checking the manuscript and the contract,' Máki says. 'We were going to meet this evening to finalise both.'

I get to my feet, and make myself another black coffee.

'That's lousy luck,' I say.

Máki looks up.

'I believe there was nothing accidental about Thorsteinn Rögnvaldsson's death,' he says bitterly.

'Meaning what?'

'I don't believe this fire was accidental.'

'No?'

He shakes his head.

'The evening after the police interrogation I called Thorsteinn,' Máki continues. 'The rule was always that he would call me and he'd use an unregistered SIM, but I felt it was so urgent to get his reactions to the police demands that I called Thorsteinn on his home number.

He told me off for using that number, but he kept his cool and we agreed to finalise everything at a meeting this evening.'

'I understand.'

'I can't help feeling that he'd still be alive if I hadn't called his home phone.'

'You realise what you're saying?' I ask sharply.

'Yes,' Máki replies. 'I suspect that my phone's been tapped and by making that call, I led them directly to my source.'

'Them? Who's them?'

'You recall as clearly as I do who it was during the interrogation who urged me repeatedly to contact my source.'

Of course. Símon Andrésson. The spooky jobsworth.

'Do you know him personally?'

'Símon was an adviser to the Minister of Justice during one Parliamentary term back in the eighties, and as a journalist I often spoke to him. I remember how fiercely loyal he was to the party and what a tough customer he could be,' Máki replies. 'When that minister had to go home with his tail between his legs after the election, Símon was appointed departmental head at the ministry and he's been there ever since. He's a through-and-through, hard-boiled party follower.'

'The law doesn't say anything about being an arsehole.'

'Símon is capable of anything, and as an influential figure within the establishment he's able to mobilise secretly the resources he certainly has.'

'He'd hardly go about setting fire to church property?'

Máki is far too downcast to notice the sarcasm in my tone.

'Guys like that have minions to do their dirty work,' he says.

'I'd urge you to not make any accusations of this nature until the autopsies have taken place and the cause of death is known.'

'An autopsy isn't going to answer the key question.'

'How the fire started?'

'Precisely.'

14

I watch that evening's news bulletins, on both stations, with more interest than usual.

Both show pictures of Thorláksbúð at Skálholt. This is a strange building of rock, turf and timber that's still standing despite the fire.

The blaze seems to have been mainly concentrated close to the ground, on the wooden cladding of the floor and the inside walls – and the altar, apparently some ancient wooden piece.

'CID is still working on establishing the cause of the fire,' a spokesman for the cops says. 'We have indications that there were burning candles inside, but at this stage it's too early to come to any conclusions. The same applies to the cause of death of the deceased. Autopsies will be carried out over the coming days.'

The evening's news bulletins lay on thick the fact that Skálholt has been the scene of personal and political tragedies in the past. The woman presenting the news spoke to a serious historian who did nothing to downplay that side of it.

'The history of the place has been closely entwined with that of the Icelandic people for the last thousand years,' he said, sounding grave. 'Skálholt was in fact the capital of Iceland for centuries, and some of the country's leading figures worked there. But Skálholt is also closely linked to some of the worst of what Icelanders have had to endure, in terms of poverty, oppression and iniquity.'

Quite an effort had gone into bringing Máki back down to earth earlier in the day, getting him to put his thoughts into a logical order. He needs to gather all the documentation he has relating to his collaboration with Thorsteinn Rögnvaldsson. That's to prepare for the coming onslaught from the city's finest. And then there's the publisher who could easily make himself scarce as soon as he hears that the main source for the book has unexpectedly left this earthly existence without signing a contract.

The TV news gives the names of the deceased.

The woman found at Thorsteinn's side in Thorláksbúð was the deacon, Jónína Katrín Nönnudóttir. She was thirty years old, unmarried and childless.

It was also mentioned that Thorsteinn had a grown-up daughter.

I search online, and get a shock.

Thorsteinn was the father of Rannveig, the TV director who dragged me up onto the Snæfellsnes glacier.

I call right away, to offer my condolences.

'Thank you,' she says, her voice quiet. 'I'm still trying to accept that Dad's dead. Everything's in a whirl in my head right now.'

'Let me know if I can help.'

'It's so unexpected. We were all there at a seminar at Skálholt on Friday and Dad had a great time.'

'Were they close, Thorsteinn and Jónína Katrín?'

'Jónína's a childhood friend of mine,' Rannveig replies. 'I hadn't noticed that she and Dad were together, and if they were, it must have been something that happened that night. But Dad had plenty of female friends after Mum died. He was always something of a Don Juan.'

'Do you have family with you now?'

'Markús is here, of course.'

'Markús?'

'Yes. My husband.'

What an idiot I can be, not knowing that Rannveig is a married woman.

'Don't forget. Call me if there's anything I can do to help.'

I head for the shower as soon as Sóley Árdís is asleep. I dry myself all over with a soft, thick towel. Then I make myself comfortable in the deepest leather armchair in the living room, with a half-full glass in my hand – naked.

I take a decent slug of the Tennessee nectar, and my mind goes over the events of the last few days.

There's the human remains on the glacier.

Then there's the turmoil around Máki, the old newshound I got to know not long after I opened my legal practice in the nineties. That's when I tried to make a living defending hoodlums and the dregs of the city.

Then Rannveig losing her father. Not that I know her all that well personally. But I like her a hell of a lot. Too well, considering she's married.

Then there are all the conversations up in the north relating to the disappearance of the young geology student from Edinburgh a decade or so ago.

Work has been piling up these last few weeks. This is the way it's often been throughout my legal career. And some of these things demand my immediate attention.

Not least the investigation into Julia MacKenzie's disappearance.

Did she turn up at Gullinhamrar on the day she vanished?

I have no idea. But the conversation at Askja between Julia and Geiri is the only new angle I've been able to uncover.

More than likely it's a straw to clutch at.

Or maybe not.

I open my laptop and write an email for Lísa Björk. I ask her to gather all the information she can about the brothers at Gullinhamrar. That's Geiri and Jósteinn – and about Alexander, the yard manager with the foreign accent.

'Please make this a complete priority for the next few days,' I write.

I'm startled by the doorbell.

I glance at my watch.

It's ten-thirty.

Who the hell dares to come calling this late in the evening?

I stand up and go to the intercom.

'Good evening.'

The voice is a familiar one. All the same, it takes a moment to connect the voice and its owner – and the name.

'Christ!' I exclaim in surprise.

'No. The Reverend Finnbogi.'

He can be as funny as fuck, I'll give him that.

'What brings you here?'

'We need to talk.'

'Then come and see me during office hours.'

'Unfortunately, I'm flying back east early tomorrow.'

'OK,' I say after thinking it over. 'I'll come down.'

I wrap myself in a pink robe, tying the belt tight. I tiptoe barefoot down the stairs. I switch on the hall light and open the door half-way.

The Reverend Finnbogi hasn't changed much since I frightened the life out of him before the altar of the old wooden church out east, right after seeing my reprobate of a father to his grave.

He's the same handsome beast, tall and strong. But he has a chiselled face, and a brightness to his eyes.

'I'm so sorry for coming so late, but I absolutely had to see you before going back east,' he apologises.

I shrug. I open the door, and close it behind us.

He fidgets in the hallway until I open the door of the meeting room on the ground floor. I switch on the light and offer him a seat by the table.

'What do you want from me?'

'It was only today that I found out you have a daughter,' he says.

'Yes. I'm a single parent. That's nothing out of the ordinary, surely?'

'I've been travelling and that's why I didn't see the interview with you about the accident on the Snæfellsnes glacier,' he says. 'My mother was adamant that I should see it.'

'Why?'

'Because she felt that your daughter resembles me,' the Reverend Finnbogi says.

'Really?'

'I looked a few things up and it turns out that she was born precisely nine months after our memorable encounter out in the east.'

'You feel that five minutes of madness in a church is something memorable?'

'Yes. I can't deny that it has often come to mind.'

I shrug.

'Our daughter has your eyes,' the Reverend Finnbogi continues.

'Do you really believe that you're her father?'

'Yes. I'm certain of it. Do you deny it?'

'Sóley Árdís is my daughter. That's all that matters.'

'It takes two.'

'Not any longer,' I shoot back. 'These days men have the same status as a stud horse. If a single woman wishes to have a child, she can simply buy semen in a foreign sperm bank. No problem.'

'But that's not what you did.'

'You know nothing about that.'

The Reverend Finnbogi doesn't seem to be amused.

'Yes. I know that, and God knows it.'

'God's not my department.'

'You came like Jezebel and seduced me in the house of the Lord,' he says. 'God knows that our coupling bore fruit, and that fruit should be a joy and a delight for us both. You have no exclusive right to our daughter.'

I sigh.

'So what is it you want, exactly?'

'I wish to see my daughter, my only child. You must understand that.'

'Go back east and take it easy,' I say, and open the meeting room door.

He sits tight.

'Is that all you have to say?'

'You knock unannounced on my door late on a Sunday evening and expect me to open my arms to you like a long-lost friend or something,' I snap. 'That's not the way it works in the real world.'

'I accept that this visit took you by surprise. Under the circumstances, I couldn't stay away.'

'I need to sleep on this for a few nights.'

The Reverend Finnbogi gets to his feet.

'Understandably, understandably. I'll be in touch shortly.'

I click the lock on the front door. Go up the stairs. I look in on my daughter, asleep in her room.

Her paternity is not registered anywhere. And it's of no importance to me.

The Reverend Finnbogi could be her father.

There are others it could have been.

Those weeks after the funeral I celebrated my new freedom from the past. There was a misunderstanding behind that. It's not as easy to bury the past as it is to bury a dead old guy. The past follows you like a shadow, all the way to the graveside.

Sóley Árdís hasn't needed a father. Not so far.

Freedom is being fatherless, as Mother said.

15

Tuesday 15th June 2010

First thing in the morning Lísa Björk hands me a slip of yellow paper.

'I'm changing my address and home phone number,' she says without any preamble.

'You're moving?'

'Ísólfur and I are going to give it a try for six months.'

'Ísólfur?'

'My boyfriend.'

This is a piece of news that comes as a surprise.

'You're really going to move in together?'

'Yes.'

'Then I hope this Ísólfur realises what a lucky man he is.'

Lísa Björk smiles.

'I just emailed you a memo.'

'Sit,' I say. 'We can go over the main points.'

She takes a seat on the red sofa next to my desk. It's under the long aerial picture of downtown Reykjavík. My old hunting ground.

Lísa Björk crosses her legs. Her attention is on her notes.

'Jósteinn and Ásgeir, known as Geiri, were both born and brought up in Sauðárkrókur. Jósteinn, the older brother, moved to Reykjavík to study. He graduated from the Hamrahlíð College and subsequently trained as an air traffic controller. He worked for many years at the international airport at Keflavík, but a few years ago he relocated to the north when he came back to Sauðárkrókur. I understand that he retired when he was around sixty and now he spends his time looking after his investments.'

'He's wealthy?'

'He appears to own a great deal of shares in funds and companies both here and overseas.'

'How did he make his money?'

'There are two stories there,' Lísa Björk says. 'Some say that he invested recklessly during the growth years, made a lot of money and managed to keep his assets somewhere safe before the financial crash in 2008. Others say he got rich while he was working in Kosovo.'

'Kosovo? In the Balkans?'

'Yes. Kosovo was part of Serbia, which was in turn part of Yugoslavia. When Yugoslavia fell apart into a bloody civil war in the nineties the Albanian population in Kosovo demanded independence and they got it after NATO bombed Serbia into obedience. The Icelandic government supported the bombing of Serbia, and subsequently provided assistance to get the government of this new country on its feet. Iceland's main contribution was to manage the construction, management and privatisation of the airport in the capital, Pristina, which was a five-year project, starting in 2004. Jósteinn was one of the Icelandic air traffic controllers who worked there during that time and I'm told that it made him a very wealthy man.'

'Aha.'

'His younger brother went in a different direction. He studied at the Hvanneyri agricultural college and graduated from there. After that he went mainly into breaking in horses, and is said to be very good at it. This took him all over the country at one time, but he's been running the stables at Gullinhamrar for more than ten years now. Jósteinn and Ásgeir leased Gullinhamrar in 1997; at that time it was in state ownership. A few years later Jósteinn set up a limited company to buy the property. This company is the sole registered owner of Gullinhamrar and Jósteinn is the sole shareholder.'

Lísa Björk flips through her notes.

'Then there's the yard manager, Alexander,' she says. 'He's an Icelandic citizen, of Kosovan origin. According to Parliamentary records, Alexander came to Iceland as a refugee from Kosovo in 1999 at the age of twenty-six. His name was Angjelo Skender Gjergji and he was a schoolteacher who lost his entire family during the war. Jósteinn gave Angjelo a job at Gullinhamrar and two years later he was granted Icelandic citizenship, and took the name of Alexander.'

'What? After two years? That's unusual.'

'Jósteinn has long had strong links to MPs in the Progressive Party, according to an old school friend who works for *Morgunblaðið*. That was the party that formed part of the government and was responsible for the Ministry of Foreign Affairs when this Kosovan refugee's citizenship was granted.'

Lísa Björk leans back on the sofa while I mull things over.

'What else do we know about Alexander's background in Kosovo?' I ask at last.

'Nothing. Except that he appears to have travelled frequently to Pristina during the years Jósteinn was working there, as an Icelandic citizen.'

'So Alexander and Jósteinn could have got up to all sorts of shady deals in Kosovo?'

'That's a possibility. I understand that criminal gangs run the place.'

'I definitely want to know more about this man's background. How about contacting the authorities in Pristina? They must have records of him, considering he was a teacher?'

'Yes, presumably. But at that time the Ministry of Education was in Serbia. I'll contact the ministries in both countries and see if they can tell us anything.'

'Sounds good.'

Lísa Björk gets to her feet.

'There's something else,' I add. 'Geiri said that they always have a few youngsters working there during the summertime. How about hunting down the kids who worked there in 2001?'

'I'll try.'

'They might remember Julia's visit.'

Lísa Björk nods.

'There's one more thing,' she says. 'When I was checking records for the family of Jósteinn and Ásgeir, I saw that they have an older half-brother living in Sauðárkrókur.'

'Anyone I ought to know?'

'You spoke to him on Saturday.'

I stare at Lísa Björk.

'Alfreð Sveinsson, who was the chief superintendent in Sauðárkrókur, has the same father as Jósteinn and Ásgeir, but a different mother.'

The old bastard!

'He could easily be concealing something his brothers might have got up to, assuming they have something to do with Julia's disappearance.'

'That's certainly a possibility.'

'You're a genius.'

Lísa Björk takes the compliment with a faint smile.

I immerse myself in everyday problems. Debts and assets. I struggle through the latest bumf from the winding-up committee of the old Landsbanki, which is still working through selling off the bankrupt bank's assets.

I was able to buy a couple of claims against the estate after the bank went bankrupt. That was when most of the overseas creditors believed that the money they had loaned to the bank was lost.

I took a chance, and bought a hundred million krónur claim for ten million.

A hell of a bargain, with hindsight.

All the indications are that I'll do very nicely out of this. That's assuming the winding-up committee ever gets round to its job of winding up the estate.

In the middle of the afternoon Lísa Björk calls through.

'There's a historian on the line, calling from America,' she says.

'What for?'

'He wants to ask you about what you found on the Snæfellsnes glacier.'

'All right. I'll talk to him.'

16

The American introduces himself as Jerome Higgins.

He says he's a professor at New York University. He's written a few books about the political history of the USA during the twentieth century.

'You can find my books on Amazon if you want confirmation of my position as an academic,' he adds.

His voice is on the hoarse side.

'What are you looking for?'

'Yesterday I read an item about what the online media over here are calling the "Ring of Death", meaning the ring you found on the glacier. The picture the police in Iceland released sparked my interest.'

'Why?'

'Because I've seen a ring with a letter L beneath a square, red stone before.'

'Really? Where?'

He clears his throat.

'Have you heard of the Loki Fellowship?'

'No, never heard of it.'

'I have investigated in some depth the covert activities of the US government during the twentieth century, and I've written both books and academic articles about this,' he says. 'The Loki Fellowship was one of the secret organisations set up by Sidney Gottlieb.'

'I've never heard of him either.'

'Gottlieb was the head of the technical arm of the US secret services when the Cold War with the Soviet Union was at its most intense, 1953 to 1972. Unfortunately for historians like me, he ensured that documents relating to extensive illegal research were destroyed shortly before he retired formally from the CIA.'

'Why was that?'

'Richard Nixon, who was President at that time, had issued a blanket ban on any further government experiments with chemical or biological weapons, and at the time investigations were just getting underway into illegal activity by the CIA. Some ruthless senior figures within the secret services took desperate measures and destroyed all of the research data that could implicate them. That's why there's so little known for certain about many of their experiments. On the other hand, information about these illegal activities came to light during Congressional inquiries, and these showed that Gottlieb had been behind several hundred illicit programmes of various kinds, often in co-operation with universities and research organisations.'

'And how does this connect to the ring?'

'It's documented that everyone engaged with the Loki Fellowship was given one of these rings.'

'So that should make it easier for the authorities to identify the body.'

'Not necessarily,' Jerome Higgins replies.

'Why not?'

'I've never seen a list of members of this organisation and seriously doubt that such a list exists.'

'Hell!'

'There's only one man who was for certain in the Loki Fellowship,' he continues in his hoarse voice. 'That's because he's mentioned in records of the secret service financial department. According to records held there, Gottlieb assigned a named subordinate the job of setting up and managing a research organisation with this name.'

'And his name?'

'This was John Adam Cussler. He was a chemical engineer and managed numerous secret research projects for Gottlieb.'

'Was? So he's dead?'

'I presume so, yes.'

'Is it possible that the body on the Snæfellsnes glacier is Cussler's?'

'That's certainly possible.'

'Are there fingerprint records held over there?'

'We can be certain that the secret services would have taken his fingerprints, as well as those of other staff.'

'I think you need to take this information to the Icelandic police.'

'It's closer to home for you to be in contact with the authorities in Iceland,' Higgins says. 'I'll send you an email with all the information available about Cussler, and you have my permission to forward this to those concerned.'

'That could work.'

'I'd appreciate it if you could keep me informed of how the investigation develops,' he continues. 'Especially if they identify the body.'

'No problem.'

Later in the day I go to fetch my daughter from nursery. On the way home we stop off at the shop to buy something for dinner.

It's nine in the evening before I get a chance to check the computer.

Jerome Higgins has sent me an email.

He describes in detail what he knows about a potential link between the Loki Fellowship research organisation and the red ring – and John Adam Cussler, the organisation's head.

I forward the information to my pal among the city's finest, fat Raggi. I urge him to get his people to check whether the frozen arm found under the ice could be Cussler's.

'You can also contact Jerome Higgins at New York University if you want all this information direct from the source,' I add.

Then I stretch out on the living room floor with my daughter, who is drawing pictures of houses and people on a white pad.

'That's our house,' she says.

'It's lovely.'

'That's me,' she continues. 'And that's Mum.'

Sóley Árdís has drawn a figure standing far away from the house.

'Is that your grandmother in another country?' I ask.

'No, that's my dad.'

She looks up at me with clear eyes.

'I have a real dad as well, don't I?' she asks in all sincerity.

17

Friday 18th June 2010

I'm busy in the office, and it's shortly before midday when my mobile buzzes across the desk for the tenth time that morning.

When I see who's calling, there's no way I'm going to reject the call.

Rannveig Thorsteinsdóttir. As delicious as a slice of cream cake.

I had told her clearly to call if she needed my help in coping with her grief.

'I need to see you right away,' she blurts out.

'What's so urgent?' I ask.

'It's too terrible to explain on the phone,' she replies. 'The world's crashing down around me.'

I can hear genuine horror and fear in her voice. Normally she's calm and totally in control.

'OK. I'll be right there.'

I pull on my leather jacket and make for the silver steed. I head out towards Seltjarnarnes where Rannveig lives with her husband in a white-painted detached house by the sea.

She answers the door dressed in black trousers and a figure-hugging white top.

Sexy.

'Come in,' she says, sweeping her long, black hair from her forehead.

She hasn't made up her face and the anguish in her brown eyes is genuine.

'What's up?' I ask as we go into the bright living room. Large prints of the films and TV programmes she has produced over the last few years hang on the walls.

Rannveig perches on the edge of a brown leather sofa. She wrings her hands in obvious desperation.

'The police are questioning Markús right now,' she says.

'What's going on?'

'We were both at a seminar at Skálholt at the weekend, and we both gave statements on Sunday morning, after Dad was found dead,' Rannveig says. 'Then the police called Markús in this morning to answer further questions and he called me just now to say they're threatening to arrest him.'

'Arrest? What for?'

Rannveig's on the verge of tears.

'The police suspect he had some involvement in Dad's death.'

Wow!

'So they don't believe the fire at Thorláksbúð was accidental?'

'I don't know anything more about what's happening,' Rannveig says. 'It was such a short call.'

'Has he admitted anything?'

'Definitely not, and these accusations sound like something completely crazy. Markús wouldn't hurt a fly and he'd no reason for any ill will towards Dad. I promised you'd help him deal with this nightmare.'

'Of course.'

I fish my phone from my pocket and call the District Commissioner's office in Selfoss. That's to let them know that I'm Markús Hálfdánarson's legal representative.

It turns out that he's being questioned at the police station in Reykjavík. That's even though the fire at Skálholt comes under the jurisdiction of the District Commissioner in Selfoss.

'I'd best get down to the police station,' I say, and get to my feet.

'Anyone who knows Markús could never imagine that he'd be involved in anything so dreadful,' Rannveig says. 'He has to be innocent!'

'This could be just a terrible mistake,' I reply. I do my best to comfort Rannveig, who's devastated.

On the way into the city, I ponder Máki's suspicion that Thorsteinn's death was most likely murder.

But what he had in mind was something other than a family tragedy.

Maybe the city's finest are barking up the wrong tree. That's happened before now. All the same, experience shows that murders are mostly committed by close friends or relatives of the victim. Booze or drugs are usually part of the picture. Or it can be a dispute over money. Occasionally it's revenge for some misdeed, real or imagined.

When good sense is switched off, the caveman instinct takes over, as Mother said.

18

The Selfoss cops aren't inclined to let me talk to Markús. They reckon they need formal confirmation that I'm his lawyer.

After some dithering, they agree to ask this new client of mine directly, and he confirms right away that he asked for my help.

Markús Hálfdánarson is around thirty. Fair-haired, slim build. His face is pale, as if he rarely sees the sun. He wears large round glasses.

I get straight to work.

'What do they have on you?'

'This is just totally ridiculous from start to finish,' he replies. 'I feel like I'm a character in a Kafka novel.'

'Rannveig said that you're suspected of involvement in the deaths of Thorsteinn and Jónína at Thorláksbúð,' I continue. 'What makes them think that?'

Markús sighs.

'It's all because I took my golf clubs with me when I went to the seminar at Skálholt,' he says after a pause. 'The police contend that they found blood on one of the clubs and they claim that it matches Thorsteinn's blood group.'

'I see. Did your father-in-law also use these clubs?'

'No. Thorsteinn and I used to play golf sometimes, but he always used his own clubs.'

'Did they find evidence of violence on the body?'

'So they say.'

'Trauma that could have been caused by a blow from a golf club?'

'That's what they say, yes.'

'They're now treating the fatalities at Thorláksbúð as murder?'

'Yes, and they seem to suspect me of being behind this terrible thing. But I had no reason to do Thorsteinn any harm. Quite the opposite. I've always got on extremely well with my father-in-law.'

'Have you denied all of these accusations during questioning?'

'Yes, of course. I haven't done anything.'

He comes across as sincere. But that doesn't mean anything.

'All right,' I say. 'I'll be present during all further questioning. If you're in any doubt, ask me before answering their questions.'

'OK.'

'Do you know why they suspect you could have wanted Thorsteinn dead?'

Markús shakes his head.

'Do they have anything else on you? Apart from the golf club?'

'Can you get me out?' he asks, desperation in his eyes, without answering my question. 'I'm dying in here.'

'At this point it's difficult to second-guess what the cops have in mind,' I say. 'I'm unaware of what aces they might yet have up their sleeves.'

'Aces?'

'They're going to continue to question you, that's for sure. That's when it'll become clear whether or not they have solid enough evidence to ask a judge to remand you in custody.'

'Custody?'

'Yes. That's the usual next step if someone is suspected of murder. The judge's decision depends on the evidence presented.'

Markús sighs out loud.

'Is there anything you'd like to tell me before we go in there? Anything I need to know about the circumstances of the case? This is so I can advise you.'

He shakes his head.

'Anything that could reflect badly on you?' I persist.

'Nothing that comes to mind,' he says in a dull voice.

'All right.'

From long experience of clients in trouble, I know that they often struggle to trust their lawyers.

Some of them even think they can get away with endless lies.

But that doesn't work out for long. Most of them find themselves tripped up over something trivial that doesn't agree with what they've already said. From then on, it's just a matter of time before the whole thing comes crashing down like any other house of cards.

Three of the boys in black are there. The one in charge has gone prematurely grey. The longstanding tribulations of life have marked his face.

'My name is Arnlaugur and I'm the chief superintendent at Selfoss,' he says, nodding to me. 'We haven't met before, as far as I know.'

He starts off slow. He asks Markús about the seminar at Skálholt, and the presentation he gave. Then about Rannveig's presentation. He discusses Markús's connections with the seminar's participants, other than family.

This includes the other victim at Thorláksbúð.

'How did you know Jónína Katrín?' Arnlaugur asks.

'Jónína was a childhood friend of my wife's,' he replies.

'She worked in Reykjavík, like you and Rannveig?'

'Yes. Jónína was a deacon and she worked extensively with sick people and others in difficult circumstances.'

'Did you often meet her?'

'We met occasionally. Jónína often visited me and Rannveig.'

Arnlaugur extracts a statement from the stack of paperwork on the table in front of the boys in black.

'We have testimony here from Jónína Katrín's elder sister,' he says. 'You're familiar with Ingunn Nönnudóttir?'

'Yes, we've met a few times.'

'She says that you and Jónína knew each other well.'

'Yes, you could say that.'

'She says that you were lovers.'

Markús turns pale and his eyes go to me.

I stare back. I can see from the look on his face that Ingunn's right.

Arnlaugur doesn't fail to notice this as well.

'When did your relationship begin?' he asks gently.

'Do I have to answer this?' Markús asks, looking at me imploringly.

I nod.

The city's finest drag out of him the details of an affair that began three years ago.

'This wasn't planned, not at all. I love my wife,' he says.

They first fell into bed together after a birthday celebration.

'Rannveig was away at a film festival in Italy on the day of the birthday party, that's why I went alone. Jónína and I shared a taxi and she invited me in, and it just happened.'

'How often did you meet?'

'Nothing more happened for many months.'

'And then?'

'We've been seeing each other pretty regularly for the last two years.'

'How regularly?'

'Every week for the first few months, normally on Wednesdays. But recently less frequently, something like a couple of times a month, maybe.'

'At Jónína's home?'

'Yes.'

'Were you in love with her?'

'Could be. But I also love my wife,' Markús replies.

I can't hide a smile.

No law of nature says you have to love one man your whole life long, as Mother said.

19

It looks like my client has been securely entangled in the police net.

They're convinced that the old green-eyed monster was behind Markús's actions at Skálholt. That summer night he had seen his lover in Thorsteinn Rögnvaldsson's company, was overcome with jealousy, followed them to Thorláksbúð armed with a golf club, beat the two of them to death and then set fire to the place to cover his tracks.

It's clear to me that the city's finest have a strong hand.

Although the autopsy reports for Thorsteinn and Jónína Katrín aren't yet available, the pathologist's preliminary finding is that they are both likely to have lost their lives due to head injuries. These injuries could have been administered using the golf club that my client confirms is his.

That alone is probably enough to earn Markús a few weeks in isolation in Litla Hraun.

When the questioning starts again, Arnlaugur asks Markús about his presence at Skálholt the evening prior to the murders.

'My presentation was on Saturday evening,' Markús replies.

'When did that finish?'

'It was certainly after ten that evening. Probably around ten-thirty.'

'Then what did you do?'

'I chatted for a while with the audience,' Markús says.

'Where?'

'First in the conference room, and then we went outside as it was such a lovely, bright summer night, and we walked up to the church.'

'When did you leave?'

'It must have been eleven, maybe even half-past.'

'Who was with you?'

'Rannveig and I went together, and her grandfather Rögnvaldur as well. He came up to Skálholt to listen to both of our presentations.'

'And Thorsteinn Rögnvaldsson? Wasn't he with you at this point?'

'Not that I recall,' Markús replies. 'We were there in groups of two or three, or a few larger groups. I wasn't paying much attention to who was where. But I recall clearly that Rannveig,

Rögnvaldur and I spoke out there on the lawn for some time before we went in to go to bed.'

'And where was Jónína Katrín?'

'I don't know.'

'Are you sure of that?'

'I don't believe she went outside until quite some time later,' Markús says.

'Were you looking for her there in the yard?'

'No. I just don't remember having seen her there.'

'Or Thorsteinn?'

Markús shakes his head.

'Did you suspect that they might be together inside the building?'

'No, not at all. I had no idea there was anything between them.'

'When did you, Rannveig and Rögnvaldur go back inside?'

'Shortly after midnight.'

'What did you do then?'

'Rannveig and I went to sleep.'

'When?'

'Around half-past midnight. Something like that.'

'Did you fall asleep right away?'

'I think so.'

'Are you sure about that?'

I can hear from Arnlaugur's tone that he has other ideas. I glance at my client, who looks despondent. He's broken emotionally, like a lamb led off to slaughter.

'Yes, I think so,' he mutters dully. He doesn't sound convincing.

The chief superintendent pulls another statement from the pile.

'We have testimony that contradicts this,' he says.

'What's that?'

'A witness claims to have seen you outside the building at roughly one o'clock.'

'May I see this statement?' I ask, as a way of giving Markús a moment's thinking time.

Arnlaugur focuses on his suspect without responding to me.

'You went outside again, didn't you? You're better off telling us the truth, my friend.'

Markús gives up.

'Yes, I went back outside,' he says. 'But I didn't harm anyone.'

'Tell us about it.'

'Rannveig fell asleep right away, but I couldn't sleep, so I got up again.'

'Where did you go?'

'I meant to meet Jónína, but she wasn't in her room.'

'So what did you do?'

'I meant to go back to bed.'

'And?'

'I ran into old Rögnvaldur in the lobby.'

'Rögnvaldur Rögnvaldsson?'

'Yes. He was getting ready to head home. I went with him out into the car park, and then went back inside and went to bed.'

'What time was this?'

'I didn't look at my watch, but I guess this must have been around one, one-thirty, something like that.'

'We know you went up to Thorláksbúð that night.'

'No. Absolutely not.'

'Did you fetch the golf club after seeing Rögnvaldur off?'

'No.'

'Or did you do that earlier?'

'I didn't touch the golf clubs that night. That's the truth.'

'Don't give me that,' Arnlaugur snaps. 'You've already admitted to being alone and not far from Thorláksbúð at around one-thirty that night. Let's hear the truth.'

'I've told you the truth.'

Arnlaugur does his best to stitch him up like a kipper, but my client's having none of it. He's adamant that he was in bed at one-thirty at the latest, and that night he met neither Jónína Katrín nor Thorsteinn – let alone did them any harm.

'Well,' the chief superintendent says as he gets to his feet. 'We're requesting an initial custody period of four weeks. You'll have plenty of time to think things over in isolation at Litla Hraun.'

I accompany my client to the court.

It doesn't take the judge long to reach a decision. He immediately approves the police request for four weeks' custody. I've nothing solid with which to sway him in the other direction. All I have is that my client denies the accusations against him.

'Tell Rannveig that I'm innocent,' Markús says as the city's finest lead him away following the ruling. 'And that I love her.'

20

I make tracks back to Seltjarnarnes.

On the way I rack my brains for a way to tell Rannveig the whole truth. That's working on the assumption she's not aware of her husband's infidelity, let alone that Markús has been jumping into the sack with Jónína Katrín on a weekly basis for the last couple of years.

But how can I explain the cops' suspicions without going into the reasoning their assertions are based on?

I pull up outside the white house. My conclusion is that it's best to answer all of Rannveig's questions honestly.

Rannveig has made up her face, as if it's a defence against the wickedness of the world. She's pinned up her hair.

'What happened?' she gasps.

'Shouldn't we sit in the living room?'

Her face goes a shade paler.

'It's that bad?'

I shut the front door behind me and lead Rannveig to the living room.

She's not alone.

An elderly man sits in one of the leather armchairs. His face is as wrinkled as the bark of an old tree. But there are still waves in his grey hair.

'This is my grandfather,' Rannveig says.

I steer her to a seat and sit at her side. I nod to Rögnvaldur Rögnvaldsson, who's planted firmly in his armchair, and offer my condolences.

So that's what he looks like. This is the man Máki is certain was behind the Icelandic government's unofficial secret service for decades during the Cold War between the Americans and the communists in the east.

'What happened?' Rannveig repeats.

'The police have Markús in custody,' I say without letting go of her arm. 'He'll be in isolation at Litla Hraun for the next four weeks.'

'God!'

I give her a moment to take it in.

Rögnvaldur clears his throat.

'What reliable evidence do they have against him?' he asks.

'Markús denies all the accusations,' I reply, looking into Rannveig's brown eyes.

'He asked me to tell you that he's innocent, and that he loves you.'

She nods her head.

'What can we do to help him?' she asks after a pause.

'All the indications are that Markús is their sole suspect and there's nobody else in the picture,' I say. 'On the other hand, I haven't seen any case files and don't know in any detail how they expect to prove his guilt. I will, of course, be present at all subsequent interrogations.'

'Is he supposed to have started the fire at Thorláksbúð?' Rögnvaldur asks.

'The cops believe that Thorsteinn and Jónína Katrín were already deceased when the fire started.'

I can see Rannveig is taken by surprise.

'They state that they have reliable suspicions of the cause of death, even though autopsies have yet to be conducted,' I continue.

'What do they think happened?'

'They are working on the assumption that Thorsteinn and Jónína both received blows to the head.'

'Fatal blows?' Rögnvaldur asks.

'Yes.'

'Do they really think that Markús beat Dad and Jónína to death?' Rannveig howls.

I hesitate for a moment, in the hope that she'll calm down.

'They believe they have the murder weapon,' I say at last.

Rannveig stares at me, wide-eyed.

'It's one of the clubs from the golf set that Markús took with him to Skálholt.'

'I can't believe it,' she says. 'Markús couldn't hit anyone, let alone with a golf club. It's not possible.'

Rögnvaldur growls again.

'While it may have been his golf club, that does not necessarily mean that Markús committed this dreadful crime,' he says. 'I walked past his golf clubs in the lobby a number of times, and everyone who attended the seminar at Skálholt would have done the same thing, many times. This proves nothing.'

'So why has Markús been arrested?' Rannveig asks, looking from one of us to the other and back.

'That should become clear in the coming days and weeks,' I

say. 'This is an investigation that's at an early stage.'

'But they must have some reason other than just that Markús had this golf club that anyone there could have stolen,' she snaps.

I glance over the dark brown coffee table at Rögnvaldur.

He gets the message right away. He pulls himself together and gets to his feet.

'I'll make us some coffee,' he says, going out into the passage. He's remarkably spry for his age.

Rannveig stares. She's waiting for an answer.

'The police are doing their damnedest to gather evidence and testimony to prove Markús's guilt,' I say.

She nods.

'A part of that is to establish a motive.'

'A motive?' she demands. 'What reason could Markús have for murdering Dad and Jónína?'

It's as clear as day that a direct, honest answer is the only option.

'They believe he did it in a fit of jealousy.'

There's nothing fake about Rannveig's astonishment.

'Jealousy?'

'Yes.'

'Is Markús supposed to have been jealous of my dad?'

'That's what they believe, yes.'

'That's just so totally crazy.'

I clasp both of Rannveig's hands in mine. I look deep into her eyes.

'Markús admitted when questioned that he and Jónína Katrín had been having an affair for some time.'

Instinct makes Rannveig laugh out loud. She stops when she sees that I'm deadly serious.

'Are you telling me that Markús has been unfaithful to me with Jónína Katrín?'

'Yes. He confirmed that.'

'With Jónína? My best friend?'

'Yes.'

Rannveig sits perfectly still for a while.

'Remember that Markús says he loves you,' I say finally. It sounds foolish.

Rannveig doesn't appear to hear me.

'You're telling me that the police believe Markús loved Jónína Katrín so much that he followed her and Dad into

Thorláksbúð that night and murdered them?' she asks.

'That's their theory,' I reply. 'Markús denies this completely.'

'But he admits the affair with Jónína?'

'Yes.'

'How long?'

I shrug.

'A month? Two months?'

'This relationship appears to have been going on for two years.'

'Two years?' she squawks. 'He's been unfaithful for two years?'

'Something like that.'

'My God,' she howls, and the tears flow unchecked. 'My God.'

I wrap my arms around Rannveig. I give her space to cry with all the rage and sorrow of a betrayed and belittled wife. I do my best to comfort her.

21

Saturday 19th June 2010

Sun, sea and sand.

No, this isn't the Costa del Sol, unfortunately. Nauthólsvík will have to do instead. The smallest bathing beach in the world, up here in the far, far north.

Sóley Árdís doesn't care.

She's busy making sandcastles. She alternates this with dips in the hot tub, where she laughs and chatters in a way that makes even the grumpiest tourist crack a smile.

It's my birthday. But it doesn't feel like anything special. Unlike last year, when I was forced against my will to turn forty.

The news of Markús Hálfdánarson's arrest for the suspected murder of his father-in-law and Jónína Katrín Nönnudóttir has spread like wildfire online. That prompted the city's finest to issue a statement to the press.

This stated clearly that the investigation is still in progress and the police are unable to elaborate on their lines of inquiry at this stage. Results of DNA tests are awaited, and as this has to be done overseas, it could take several weeks.

Máki called last night. He wanted to ask about my client, who is adamant that he's innocent.

The old newshound was almost elated, having instinctively sensed that his source had been murdered. But he's certain that the police are on the wrong track.

'I'm absolutely positive that Thorsteinn's death is a direct consequence of his revelations during his conversations with me,' he said.

'The cops make a habit of arresting innocent people,' I say.

'I know for sure that those who make the decisions behind closed doors in the Icelandic power system must have seen Thorsteinn as a dangerous whistle-blower,' Máki said. 'He wanted the country to know about the establishment's shady activities during the Cold War, and they won't see that as anything less than treason.'

Sóley Árdís has had enough of paddling. For the moment, at any rate.

She trots over to me, clutching her little yellow bucket and spade, and sets about building a sandcastle on a palatial scale.

'Thorsteinn told me that some of his old comrades would undoubtedly react furiously to his revelations,' Máki continued. 'But to tell the truth, he was more concerned about losing old friends and acquaintances when the book came out, rather than threats and enmity from establishment figures.'

'Well, I imagine they would take that kind of betrayal very personally.'

'He told me more than once that the worst part of it was letting down friends, betraying those who for years on end had trusted him with confidences and secrets. I think that Thorsteinn had decided to expose all these secret political machinations for his own peace of mind, some kind of penance for the sins of the past.'

'I will naturally continue to stress that there are others who had stronger motives than Markús to seek revenge on Thorsteinn.'

'Exactly.'

'But whoever did this has to be one of the relatively few people who were present at Skálholt that night.'

'Or part of the night. He could have arrived after midnight, seen Thorsteinn and Jónína Katrín disappear into Thorláksbúð, and taken the opportunity.'

'You're forgetting that the killer must have seen the golf clubs in the reception area of the school where the seminar was held,' I reply. 'That means he must have been in there before the murder was committed.'

'Or an accomplice.'

'Yes, possibly. If there are two perpetrators.'

That evening, when Sóley Árdís is asleep in her room, I sit with my laptop and scour the online world for the latest news and opinions on the Skálholt murders. I see that the city's finest must have leaked the love triangle angle to their friends in the media. At least, one outlet carries the assertion that the murdered man and the suspected murderer had both been involved with the same woman. The comments show that some people see this as amusing. Others are outraged that the media are heaping scandal on people who've already been hurt.

It's not as if any of this takes me by surprise. There are plenty of people who will say anything in online comments, frequently totally irresponsible stuff.

I just hope that Rannveig has the sense to avoid the internet while the storm's raging. She has enough problems as it is.

I'm still deep in the online crap when Rannveig calls shortly before midnight.

'I'm sorry, Stella,' she says. 'I can't sleep.'

'No problem,' I reply. 'You can call me whenever you like.'

It's her husband's infidelity that's uppermost in her mind.

'It's unbelievable that I didn't notice anything,' she sobs. 'I keep thinking over our life together for the last couple of years and there's nothing that should've warned me he'd been fucking my best friend. Sex had become something of a routine, but we always did it when he wanted. I never said no, so it's not as if that's what drove him to her.'

'The only reasonable explanation for infidelity in general is the craving for variety,' I say. 'I understand from what Markús said that he loved you both. Sometimes that's the way it is.'

'I visited her sister today,' Rannveig continues.

'Ingunn?'

'According to her, Jónína told her about the relationship last Christmas. Jónína told her that she felt deeply guilty for having betrayed me.'

'Then shouldn't she have broken it off? If she felt so bad about it?'

'Ingunn thinks that Jónína wanted to break it off,' Rannveig replies. 'That's the only explanation for why she went out with Dad that night.'

'Who knows?'

Rannveig sighs heavily down the phone.

'Is there anyone with you tonight?' I ask after a long silence.

'No. Grandad went home yesterday evening, but he'll be back in town on Monday to help me organise the funeral.'

'Have you set a day for it?'

'Grandad suggested a week on Saturday. I'll leave that up to him.'

Rannveig sighs.

'When are you meeting Markús next?' she asks.

'After the weekend. Tuesday or Wednesday.'

'Do you still believe he's innocent?'

'As a lawyer, I always work on the assumption that my client is telling the truth. Even when their accounts seem to be at odds with the facts.'

'As in this case?'

'I wouldn't like to say at this stage,' I reply. 'To my mind a key aspect of this is that the police have failed to prove that

Markús was at Thorláksbúð that night. As things stand, I have to treat all their suspicions as being based on conjecture.'

'In spite of everything, I want to believe that Markús is innocent,' Rannveig says. 'But maybe I don't know him anywhere near as well as I thought I did.'

'There's a world of difference between infidelity and murder.'

'Yes, I know. But maybe I'm just so blinkered.'

I can hear the doubts taking hold in her mind.

That comes as no surprise. And it could make the next stage of the game easier for me, if everything turns out for the worst.

Doubt is the route to truth, as Mother said.

22

Monday 21st June 2010

Lisa Björk gets the week off to a flying start.

'I managed to find a lad who worked a summer at Gullinhamrar in 2001,' she says as soon as I appear in the office.

'Brilliant!'

'His name's Birkir Brynjólfsson and he was a stable boy for Geiri at Gullinhamrar in 2000 and 2001. He now works in a garage in Kópavogur.'

She hands me a yellow Post-it with the garage's details.

'I haven't contacted him,' she adds. 'I expected you'd prefer to speak to him directly.'

'Quite right.'

I grab the phone and call the garage. I speak to Birkir and ask him to come to my office as soon as possible. I don't give him a reason.

My request takes him completely by surprise.

He stammers and hesitates, as if he expects the worst from the legal profession. Finally, he agrees to stop by in his lunch break.

Lísa Björk shows him into the meeting room. She gives him a bottle of pop and some chocolate biscuits.

Birkir is dark-haired. He's short and chubby, doesn't look like a pleasant character.

He comes across as insecure, hesitant.

I try to be friendly, to show him that he has nothing to fear from me.

'Have you been working with cars for long?' I ask.

'I started working at a garage back home in Sauðárkrókur,' he replies. 'But I'm mostly working on motorbikes.'

'Ah? Bikes are your speciality?'

'I've always enjoyed tinkering with them.'

'You have a bike of your own?'

'Yeah, I've had several. But right now I have a 2006 Harley Davidson Road King.'

'That's a cool bike?'

'Absolutely fantastic.'

I reach for my laptop. I pull up the photo of Julia and Geiri taken at Askja. I show Birkir the screen.

'What can you tell me about that bike?'

He peers at the picture.

'Looks like a Kawasaki GTR1000,' he says after a moment's thought. 'Could be a 1994 or 1995 model.'

'You know pretty much everything about motorcycles?'

'Bikes are both my job and my main interest,' Birkir says, and smiles shyly.

'This photo was taken at Askja,' I continue. 'The girl's name is Julia MacKenzie and she's there in the picture with Geiri from Gullinhamrar. You worked for Geiri for a couple of summers, didn't you?'

'Yeah. Two summers.'

'You were there during the summer of 2001?'

He nods.

'Do you remember seeing this girl there in July 2001?'

Birkir's eyes go back to the screen. He scratches the back of his neck.

'I remember a foreign girl on that type of bike who came to see Geiri,' he replies at last. 'She even let me have a go on the bike.'

'Was it this girl?'

'I never knew what her name was. But she definitely rode that type of bike.'

'And that was July 2001?'

'I'm pretty sure it was,' Birkir says. 'I worked for Geiri through June and July both summers, and that was just before I left.'

'Do you remember what Julia did at Gullinhamrar? Apart from giving you a go on her motorcycle?'

'I think she went out riding.'

'She can hardly have gone out on horseback alone in an unfamiliar place?'

'I think Geiri's brother offered to go with her.'

'Did Jósteinn often go out with groups on horseback?'

Birkir grins.

'Sometimes,' he says. 'If he wasn't too drunk.'

'He was often drunk?'

'He'd have long binges. He used to drink for days at a time.'

'He drank alone?'

'Sometimes Alexander would drink with him, and sometimes they'd have a woman with them.'

'And Geiri?'

'No. Geiri never touched a drop. I remember Jósteinn teasing him once that he couldn't handle booze or women.'

'Was Jósteinn drunk when he went riding with Julia?'

Birkir shrugs.

'And do you know where they rode?'

'No. I was taking a group of kids on horseback up to Tíndastóll, and they must have gone in the other direction.'

'Did you see Julia again after that day?'

'No.'

'And did you see her motorcycle again?'

'No. Didn't see that either.'

'So she was gone by the time you came back with the youngsters?'

'I didn't see either her or her bike again after I went out with that group. That's for sure.'

'And Jósteinn?'

'What about him?'

'Did you see him again after that day?'

'I don't remember, but he was there at Gullinhamrar the last few days I was working for Geiri.'

'Are you prepared to sign a statement to that effect?'

'I don't see why not,' he replies after hesitating for a moment, and he signs in my and Lísa Björk's presence.

'What now?' she asks once he's gone.

'We have evidence that places Julia at Gullinhamrar on the day she disappeared,' I reply. 'On the basis of new evidence, we can demand that a new investigation be carried out into her disappearance, and that's what I'm going to do.'

23

Wednesday 23rd June 2010

Máki lets rip on *News Blog* this morning.

The Ring of Death and the Loki Fellowship
Is the body in the glacier a CIA spy?

The article is based largely on his interview with Jerome Higgins, the NYU professor.

I put him on the trail. It's a way of putting pressure on the city's finest. The relationship between me and Máki is based on a solid foundation of mutual interest. He's always looking for fresh news. I make use of that to put into the public arena the odd story that helps in my war with the establishment.

Máki mentions in the opening of the article the widespread illegal research and experiments conducted by the US secret services during the Cold War. But he places greater emphasis on the professor's account of John Adam Cussler, the Loki Fellowship membership ring and the possibility that the head of this secret research outfit came to Iceland in the summer of 1973.

'According to *News Blog*'s reliable sources, the FBI is currently checking the fingerprints of the hand found on the Snæfellsnes glacier against records they hold of Cussler's fingerprints,' Máki concludes.

I glance at my watch. I'm running late.

Two meetings ahead of me this afternoon.

The first is in just forty minutes at the police station in Selfoss. That's where I'm going to try to give Chief Superintendent Arnlaugur a run for his money. Right after that I'll have to make tracks for Litla Hraun for a chat with Markús Hálfdánarson.

I skip lunch and get going.

Arnlaugur has dragged his feet sending me copies of the police reports concerning the murder at Thorláksbúð. He tries to tell me they aren't ready. He also said I need be in no hurry getting this stuff, as my client's situation isn't going to change in the next few weeks.

But I don't relax the pressure on him.

His office is a stone's throw from the banks of the Ölfus river.

He's perfectly polite. He repeats the force's apologies, and hands me a couple of reports.

'In this folder are the description of the scene at Thorláksbúð and the pictures our forensics guys took,' he says. 'There's also a copy of your client's statement and the testimony of three key witnesses who were aware of his movements that night.'

I take the folder, and flip quickly through the contents.

'That's a good start,' I say.

'Hopefully, your client will come round to the idea that truth is the best story to tell,' Arnlaugur adds.

'Those who know Markús Hálfdánarson consider him incapable of such violence,' I reply.

'I don't doubt that your client is as gentle as a lamb under normal circumstances,' the chief superintendent says. 'But my experience in this job is that even the most placid of men can unfortunately lose control when passion takes over.'

By now my belly really is demanding food.

I notice a small café near the bridge over the Ölfus river. I'm in there. I shovel down a chicken salad as I take a closer look at the folder.

Thorsteinn's and Jónína's bodies were naked on the floor.

The remains of their discarded clothes lay here and there each side of the bodies, which were burned to some extent.

The forensic team believes the fire didn't start until well into the night. That could have been as late as just one hour before the door was opened.

They expect that the two large candles that stood on the floor before the altar must have burned right down, until Thorláksbúð's wooden floor caught fire.

But the murders had clearly been committed some time earlier. Most likely around two in the morning.

This presumably means that the murderer was long gone by the time the fire took hold of the building's timber cladding.

The forensics people have also identified the murder weapon. It's a Galloway number seven, found in the grass to the east side of the church.

That's exactly the club that was missing from my client's golf bag. That's no surprise, as there's no argument about whether or not the golf club is his. The question is who used it to beat Thorsteinn and Jónína to death in Thorláksbúð.

The absence of fingerprints on the club is remarkable.

That indicates that the murderer went calmly about his work.

He must have had the presence of mind to wipe his own prints from the murder weapon. And those of anyone else, including my client's.

Markús is in a desperate state when I finally get to see him in the narrow little meeting room at Litla Hraun. That's after I've been meticulously patted down.

'Until now I'd never have believed what a shock it is to be ripped away from your usual surroundings and isolated from everything and everyone you know,' he says. 'I've read books about others undergoing this kind of experience, but was totally unprepared for this.'

'You get used to it.'

'I might just as well be dead,' he added morosely. 'My reputation is wrecked, and so is everything else I value in life, even if they manage to prove my innocence.'

'You're still alive,' I retort. 'And self-pity's not going to help.'

Markús buries his face in his hands.

'You need to tell me the whole truth,' I add.

'Everything I tell you is the truth.'

'You tried to conceal your affair with Jónína Katrín. It's not clever to tell lies to your lawyer.'

'I thought nobody knew about us.'

'I want to go over that Saturday at Skálholt again. You up for that?'

He places his hands flat on the table. He nods.

'Did you suspect that Thorsteinn was after Jónína that night?'

'They sat together at dinner,' Markús said after a long pause for thought. 'I was surprised at how long Thorsteinn had been pursuing Jónína, but she always turned him down.'

'How do you know?'

'She told me herself. But I noticed that she behaved differently with him that evening.'

'Different – how?'

'He whispered a lot to her, made her laugh.'

'When was it that you were sure they were together?'

'That was after midnight when I went to her room and found that she wasn't in bed.'

'What did you do then?'

'I sneaked up to Thorsteinn's door, but didn't dare knock.'

'Then what?'

'I went back to Rannveig, but couldn't get to sleep so I went out and ran into Rögnvaldur, just as I said during the interrogation.'

'When did it occur to you that Thorsteinn and Jónína were screwing in Thorláksbúð?'

'It didn't. I thought they were in his room together.'

'Were you jealous?'

'I felt very uncomfortable that night. My feelings were very odd and contradictory. I think it was some combination of jealousy and anger, as well as a bitter guilt at having betrayed Rannveig. I lay awake and didn't get to sleep until it was almost morning.'

I lean forward.

'Tell me the whole truth,' I say, staring into his eyes. 'Did you go into Thorláksbúð that night?'

'No, no, and again no,' he protests angrily. 'I admit I committed adultery, but I'm innocent of this foul crime.'

24

Rannveig Thorsteinsdóttir's wearing nothing more than tight denim shorts and a sleeveless black T-shirt.

Sweet!

She opens the door without a word. She marches back down the broad staircase leading to the basement of the house.

I shut the front door behind me and follow her down to the studio that bristles with computers, screens of all sizes and all sorts of other equipment.

She's been going through footage on the largest screen. That's our trip up to the Snæfellsnes ice cap.

'I had to get back to work,' she says by way of explanation. 'I was going crazy with worry and anger, and doing nothing wasn't helping.'

'It doesn't do any harm to keep busy.'

She sits in a black chair and pulls her feet up under her.

'You saw Markús?'

'Yes. I've come straight from Litla Hraun.'

'How's he feeling?'

'The first few days on remand are always very tough. Especially for an innocent man.'

'Is Markús innocent?'

'Innocent of murder, he says. But guilty of adultery. He's rock solid on this.'

'What happens next?'

'The police are waiting for the DNA results from the blood on the golf club. If that shows it's the murder weapon, as we can expect, then it's likely that Markús will be charged with the murders. It seems obvious that they're not looking for anyone else. But whether the evidence is strong enough for a prosecution and a conviction is another matter altogether.'

'Why's that?'

'According to the reports I have from the Selfoss police, there are no fingerprints on the golf club,' I say. 'On top of that, practically everyone who was at the seminar at Skálholt knew that Markús's golf clubs were there in the lobby, as they were there for anyone to see. As far as I know, none of the witnesses report having seen Markús anywhere near Thorláksbúð that night, or even going in that direction. The witnesses who observed him in the yard between one and two that night were asked specifically if they recalled him having a golf club in his hand, but none of them remember seeing that. All that serves to weaken the state's case significantly.'

Rannveig sits motionless. She's deep in thought.

'I think the worst possible outcome would be for us to never know the truth,' she says, a worried look on her face. 'That would be dreadful.'

'If Markús is innocent, then someone else has to be guilty,' I reply. 'Someone who was at the seminar. We can hardly expect it to be anyone else.'

Rannveig nods.

'How many people were there that Saturday?'

'There were twenty-two participants in the seminar, including the introductory speakers.'

'So there are twenty people who are suspects. Seventeen, if we discount your family. That's not a big group.'

Rannveig gets to her feet and marches over to a desk at the far end of the studio. She hurriedly leafs through a stack of paperwork, and finds what she's looking for.

'Here's the list of the seminar participants.'

She hands me the list and sits back on her big boss chair.

At the top of the page it says *God in the Movies*.

'Was that the topic?' I ask.

'Yes. We were examining the various portrayals of God through the history of film,' Rannveig replies.

I glance down the list. A lot of them are priests and theologians.

'How many of them spoke on the Saturday?'

'Örnólfur Indriðason was the first speaker, on concepts of faith in film versions of Icelandic books, everything from *Sons of the Soil* to *Christianity Beneath the Glacier*.'

'Aha.'

'I spoke in the afternoon. My presentation was about the portrayal of God in Icelandic movies over the last thirty years, or since the beginning of what we call the Icelandic film wave.'

'And Markús?'

'He spoke in the evening with a presentation about a variety of foreign films that are based directly on the Bible. There were two more presentations scheduled for the Sunday, but of course they were cancelled.'

I open my russet-brown briefcase. I tuck the list of names inside it.

The image of me and Rannveig is still on the big screen. I get an idea.

'Did you film anything at Skálholt that Saturday?' I ask.

Rannveig looks around.

'Yes. With my iPad.'

She feeds the images from the tablet onto the big screen.

Together we watch some short, random clips. Some were recorded at the seminar. Others are of people chatting during the coffee and meal breaks, indoors and out.

Rannveig freezes one clip on the screen.

It shows Thorsteinn and Jónína Katrín sitting together at the dinner table.

They're both laughing.

They're a pair of happy victims enjoying life, just a few hours before their unexpected appointment with death at Thorláksbúð.

Thorsteinn looks up, directly at the lens. It's as if he's saying something to his daughter.

Rannveig stifles a sob.

Thorsteinn was undeniably a handsome man, even though he was pushing sixty. He's tall and well built, with dark hair and lively eyes.

A real Don Juan.

Jónína Katrín appears in many respects to be his complete opposite. Not only is she half Thorsteinn's age, she's also petite and delicate.

'I so rarely saw Dad after he moved to the Westman Islands,' Rannveig says with a sob at the back of her throat. 'When I went to study abroad, we used to catch up sometimes on Skype, but we only met maybe two or three times a year.'

The phone interrupts.

Rannveig snatches up her phone. She yesses a few times and ends the call.

'My grandfather's coming,' she says. 'We have to go and meet the priest.'

'All right,' I say, getting to my feet. 'I'll let you know if anything new turns up.'

25

Saturday 26th June 2010

The day before yesterday I formally delivered to the National Police Commissioner's office my written request for a new investigation into the disappearance of Julia MacKenzie in the summer of 2001. This was accompanied by a detailed outline of new information that makes it essential to reopen the case.

At the same time, I presented a demand that the investigation should be carried out by the National Police Commissioner, and not the District Commissioner in Sauðárkrókur. The reasoning I put forward is that the Sauðárkrókur police had failed to interview Chief Superintendent Alfreð Sveinsson's half-brothers, even though both Geiri and Jósteinn had met Julia before she disappeared.

I had a chat with Fat Raggi while I was there. Told him about it, and asked him to let me know what the outcome might be. I reminded him that Julia's mother didn't have long to live.

He looked thoughtful when I mentioned Alfreð Sveinsson's involvement.

'I never heard anything bad about Alfreð,' he said.

'I've no special interest in stirring up trouble for him,' I replied. 'But it's clear that Julia's trail doesn't come to an end in Sauðárkrókur, as had been assumed, but at Gullinhamrar where his half-brothers rule the roost.'

This morning I wondered whether or not to attend the funeral of Thorsteinn Rögnvaldsson, someone I didn't know at all.

I decided to go. Sóley Árdís was deposited with Cora and my cousin Sissi. Then I made for Seltjarnarnes where the funeral took place.

I'm not kidding myself. I know exactly why I took the time and trouble. I gaze longingly at Rannveig walking through the church behind her father's coffin.

She looks stunning in black.

A few years ago I was in her position. That was back on the old home turf in the east. That's where I stood over the husk of my father.

But I wore white. As if I wanted to dance on his grave. He deserved that.

In spite of everything, Rannveig is fortunate. She had a father she loved. He's someone she can grieve in all sincerity.

I imagine she knows little or nothing about his old secrets, Thorsteinn's political snooping for Rögnvaldur Rögnvaldsson back in the seventies – the betrayals of his comrades who believed him to be one of them.

Was Thorsteinn a wolf in sheep's political clothing? Or was he an unwitting pawn on his father's chessboard as he seemed to wage a holy war against anything that he referred to as communist?

I don't know.

My suspicion is that Máki's narrative around Rögnvaldur Rögnvaldsson's secret activities is seriously exaggerated. But I notice a good many elderly types who are there to offer the old man their condolences at the wake in the church hall. They come up to him one after another. They sit before him like dutiful disciples.

I recognise many political figures in the gathering. Most I've only seen as faces on TV. There are also big hitters from the world of business, and a few cultural icons. Some of them are no doubt there because of their friendship with Rannveig, who makes a point of passing through the throng of guests and thanking them for their sympathy.

Apart from that, wakes like these get on my nerves.

The outright hypocrisy that hovers in the air above the excellent refreshments in the name of the deceased and the appetites of the mourners never fail to get on my nerves. They're the ones celebrating being still above ground.

Rannveig isn't going to let me go right away.

'My grandfather would like to speak to you,' she says as I'm about to leave.

I go to the table where Rögnvaldur sits. I don't take a seat facing him, but stand at the old man's side. It's as if I'm demonstrating that we stand equal.

'Rannveig is under terrible pressure, but she's bearing up well,' he says in a voice that's hoarse.

'Understandably. It's not easy for her to lose her father in this way. And her husband's in prison.'

'I notice that you're willing to help her through the worst of her difficulties.'

'She's worth it.'

'We are in agreement on that.'

Rögnvaldur turns to me.

'Her marriage is naturally at an end, even though she doesn't appear to have fully grasped it,' he says.

'Are you certain of that?'

'Rannveig won't hear of divorcing Markús as things stand,' he continues. 'That's out of some mistaken loyalty to her husband who's in a difficult situation. As time passes, she'll understand that a divorce is the only solution for the future. But I accept that it'll take some time for that to sink in. Many people see a divorce as a defeat.'

'Why are you telling me this?'

'I deem it fitting that you have the right impression.'

'Do you believe that Markús murdered your son?'

I'm struck by how Rögnvaldur chooses not to answer my direct question.

'My chief concern is that Rannveig should have a clear resolution,' he says. 'Doubt is tearing her apart.'

'Don't you have close friends within the justice system?' I ask, looking into the old man's eyes. 'Influential people who can pull strings?'

'My influence doesn't extend as far as it once did.'

'I've heard tales of the power you've wielded behind the scenes.'

'There were times during the height of the Cold War when my opinions were listened to.'

'Reds under the bed, and all that?' I ask with a smile.

'You young people have no conception of how serious the situation was at one time,' Rögnvaldur replies. 'We stood for years on the front line, day after day, to defend this country and its people. This is why Iceland is a free democracy.'

He clears his throat.

'But that's by the way,' he adds. 'There's something else I wanted to tell you.'

'What's that?'

'I dropped in to see my son that Saturday evening at Skálholt. This was shortly after Markús had finished his presentation at the seminar.'

'And?'

'Örnólfur Indriðason was arguing with Thorsteinn in his room as I approached the door. I could hear them from out in the corridor.'

'Örnólfur? Didn't he give a presentation earlier in the day?'

'Yes.'

'What was their argument about?'

'I couldn't make out what was said, except when Örnólfur called my son a "fucking traitor" and stormed out.'

I look steadily into the old man's eyes.

'Are you making up something to help Markús?' I ask.

'It's the truth of the matter,' Rögnvaldur says. 'I have already made a statement to Arnlaugur to this effect.'

'Is this Örnólfur here?'

'He appears to be saying goodbye to Rannveig.'

I turn to look.

Örnólfur is short and thin. He has a long, dark beard.

'Did Thorsteinn mention why Örnólfur was so angry with him?'

'My last conversation with my son was of a deeply personal nature and has no bearing on his death.'

'Are you sure of that?'

'I understand that Arnlaugur intends to look more closely into Örnólfur's movements during the night my son died,' Rögnvaldur continues. 'But you also need to do everything in your power to direct the attention of the police and the media in other directions, for instance by leaking this new information, but without mentioning my name in connection with it.'

I can only smile at the old guy's cunning. It's obvious that he's no stranger to pulling this kind of trick. That's regardless of whether or not what he's saying is true.

But I mustn't underestimate the old fox – and definitely not trust him to be telling the truth.

What's most important is to not lie to yourself, as Mother said.

26

The professor in New York has sent me a new email.

'I've hardly had a moment's peace from the US media since the interview with me appeared on an Icelandic news website, which demonstrates once again just how small the online world is,' Jerome Higgins writes.

'There's been an incredible interest in the ring that was found on the Snæfellsnes glacier because of the possible link to John Adam Cussler. While many find it hard to believe that he met his end there on the ice, nobody can deny that 'the ring of death' bears a close resemblance to the one Cussler used as the emblem of those who worked for the Loki Fellowship research organisation. Pictures don't lie.'

Higgins continues with the information he has at his disposal relating to the CIA's secret research activity.

'According to the sources I've been able to track down within the government here, this research outfit was set up in 1954. For many years it was based on the sixth floor of building number 470 at Fort Detrick, a well-known US Army base in Virginia, but was moved elsewhere in 1971, just before Nixon confirmed the ban on further research of this nature. I have a document with the names of three assignments this organisation was working for on Sidney Gottlieb's behalf. These are BERSERK, BIFROST and RAGNAROK. It is interesting that these names are all drawn from Germanic mythology. On the other hand, I have no knowledge of the subjects of this research, as all of the relevant files were destroyed in 1972.'

Higgins adds that he has seen a photocopy of a report that relays a conversation between an FBI agent and Cussler in August 1972.

'It appears that the FBI were investigating the illegal destruction of documents concerning secret service activities by Sidney Gottlieb and his staff. It is stated that no documents were found during a covert search of Cussler's hotel room in Germany. Also that during the meeting, Cussler flatly refused to answer the agent's questions.'

The most recent information Higgins has concerning Cussler dates back to 1973.

'In the early part of that year he was in Greenland and intended to continue to Iceland in the spring. It is uncertain whether or not he came to Iceland, but it is confirmed that he intended to travel there shortly before the meeting of the US and French Presidents in Reykjavík in the summer of 1973. Cussler's final activity and what became of him have been shrouded in secrecy for decades. That's why I'm hoping that what you found on the glacier are his remains.'

The ring of death.

To my mind, this name the media dreamed up is ridiculous.

But it goes without saying that I've no idea, any more than the American professor does, of whether Cussler came to Iceland in the spring of 1973, or what could have brought him here. For that matter, I've no idea if the ring I stumbled across up on the glacier is his, or if it came from a jewellery shop on Laugavegur, right here in Reykjavík.

The truth of it is that I don't really care. Solving this riddle isn't my headache, even though I was the one who breathed life into it.

I've more than enough on my plate these days with other urgent work. At the top of the list is to search for every possible way to clear my client of the city's finest's suspicions that he committed the murder at Skálholt. Second on the list is doing everything I can to pressure the cops into tracing Julia MacKenzie's movements after she arrived at Gullinhamrar. Number three is to stand guard over the Stella Fund.

In the afternoon I fetch Sóley Árdís from Cora and my cousin Sissi. The weather's fine so we take a walk together. Check out a couple of shops without buying anything. On the way back we treat ourselves to ice cream.

I still haven't decided what to do about the Reverend Finnbogi's request. My instinct is to keep him away from my daughter.

Why should I let this man of God into our lives?

I don't know him at all, even though our meeting in passing resulted in this unexpected and delightful outcome.

All the same, I'm uncertain.

Sooner or later, Sóley Árdís is going to ask me who her father is.

What then?

What will her reaction to my secrecy be when she's in her teens? Will she blame me for not allowing her father to be a part of her childhood?

That means eliminating the uncertainty. Make her paternity clear.

Sheesh!

What's going on with all this Hamlet shit? I've always been quick to take decisions. Right or wrong.

Deep down, I know why I'm dithering like the doubtful Danish prince.

It's simply because it's my daughter's welfare that's at stake.

Máki calls after the evening TV news.

'How was the funeral?' he asks, straight to the point.

'Are you hunting for news?'

'Always on the hunt for news.'

'You don't quote a single word of mine about the funeral.'

'Agreed.'

I answer a few questions of his about the service and the guests at the wake. But this is an opportunity for me to learn something.

'What can you tell me about Örnólfur Indriðason?'

He instantly pricks up his ears.

'Why this interest in the Eagle?'

'Eagle?'

'Örnólfur was always called the Eagle back when he was fighting for a revolution in Iceland,' Máki replies.

'He was one of the speakers at the seminar at Skálholt when the murder was committed,' I say. 'He was also at the funeral and the wake.'

'That's no surprise. He and Thorsteinn were childhood friends and comrades in the Movement in the sixties and seventies.'

'What Movement?'

'The Movement was a collection of all sorts of communists and the first group of that kind here to adopt Trotskyism.'

'What sort of ism is that?'

'You must have heard of Trotsky?'

'I've heard the name.'

Máki's in his element whenever he gets a chance to explain tortuous political machinations.

'Trotsky was one of the leaders of the Russian revolution in 1917,' he says. 'You know. The revolution that led to the formation of the Soviet Union.'

'Yep. I've heard of that.'

'One of his main messages was that the revolution never ends, meaning that the revolution continues as an endless process. That didn't go down well with Stalin who took power in the Soviet Union. He hounded Trotsky out of the country and had him assassinated in Mexico. But Trotsky's theories had a life of their own with the Fourth International, and the Movement was part of that political outfit back in the seventies, but it fizzled out around 1980, if I remember correctly.'

'So Thorsteinn and Örnólfur were Trotskyists?'

'Exactly. Thorsteinn mentioned Örnólfur a few times while we were working on the book. Apart from that, it's amusing to see that some of the Trots, as they were called, have made themselves very comfortable in the bourgeois society that they wanted to overturn when they were youngsters. Take the Central Bank as an example. It's managed mainly by old revolutionaries from the Movement. Unbelievable, but true.'

'Örnólfur's hardly battling for revolution in Iceland?'

'I don't think so. He's a teacher and specialises in film studies, and no longer has anything to do with politics. At least, not publicly.'

I decide to not tell Máki about the argument between Örnólfur and Thorsteinn at Skálholt. First I'd like to hear from Arnlaugur in person that there's new testimony from Rögnvaldur Rögnvaldsson.

The old man could easily be trying to put one over on me.

Villains are always a step ahead of honest people, as Mother said.

27

Sunday 27th June 2010

I make a call to the east at dinner time.

Over the phone, the Reverend Finnbogi is unable to conceal his disgust.

'You went with many men at the same time?' he demands.

'I don't need any damned lectures on morality from a priest who allows himself to fuck women on the altar,' I reply coldly. 'But if you're prepared to let me have a DNA sample that I can have compared to my daughter's, then I'm prepared to carry out a paternity test. If not, then this matter's closed as far as I'm concerned.'

'Of course I want to be certain,' the man of God replies.

'Let me know next time you're in town,' I tell him, and end the call.

Later that evening I make myself comfortable in the living room with my laptop. I plug in the memory stick Rannveig gave me. Her recordings from the Skálholt seminar appear on the screen.

I freeze the replay of Örnólfur Indriðason. He's the bearded film specialist who gave the first presentation on the Saturday. That was something about God in films based on Icelandic novels.

Örnólfur isn't exactly a wimp, but close to it. He doesn't look like he has the strength for any kind of a fight.

But I can't let appearances deceive me. There are examples that prove fury and jealousy can turn the puniest nerd into a killer.

Another sequence recorded outdoors shows Thorsteinn Rögnvaldsson walk up from the car park and greet Markús, shaking his hand.

On the last day of his life, Thorsteinn looks lively and cheerful. He's wearing a light-coloured suit with a white shirt. There's a small, dark red briefcase in his right hand.

Documents?

I freeze the image on the screen.

Thorsteinn was a guest at the seminar, not a speaker.

So why arrive with a briefcase?

Máki's words on the day the bodies were discovered at Thorláksbúð come back to me.

Thorsteinn was checking the manuscript and the contract. We were going to meet this evening to finalise both.

Could the manuscript have been in the briefcase? Along with the draft contract?

I call Rannveig. She sounds down.

'I feel lousy,' she says.

'Come over to my place. I have the best cure there is for sorrow.'

She hesitates.

'Sorrow is something that it's not good to deal with alone,' I add.

After a lot of persuasion, Rannveig allows herself to be convinced.

Half an hour later she's sitting on the leather sofa in my living room. She's still wearing the black dress.

I fetch a fresh bottle of Jack D and fill a couple of shot glasses.

'We're drinking this neat?' she asks.

'Of course,' I reply with a smile. 'It's bordering on treason to mix something like this with anything else.'

'I'm not much given to spirits.'

'One, two, three!'

I knock back my drink.

She hesitates, and then sips.

'Down the hatch!'

Rannveig obeys.

'God, that's powerful,' she says.

'It comes with practice.'

I refill the glasses.

Rannveig looks sadly at the picture on the computer screen.

'The last time I hugged Dad was in the car park at Skálholt.'

'Thorsteinn has a red-brown briefcase there. Any idea what happened to it?'

She shakes her head.

'You haven't received the belongings he had with him at Skálholt?'

'No. I guess the police still have it all.'

'Probably.'

She stares with sorrow in her eyes at the picture of her father.

'How well do you know Örnólfur Indriðason?' I ask.

'He's one of my father's oldest friends,' Rannveig replies.

'But do you know him well?'

'He often called on us out at Seltjarnarnes when I was little. I also went to his lectures on the history of film before I went on to study film.'

'Does he have a temper?'

She shrugs.

'Were they good friends?'

'As far as I know. Why do you ask?'

'According to your grandfather, there was an argument between Örnólfur and Thorsteinn at Skálholt.'

'About what?'

'He couldn't make out what they were saying.'

'Is that conversation important?'

'Your grandfather says that Örnólfur was genuinely furious with your father. So that means there are questions about his actions that night.'

A gleam of new hope lights up her eyes.

'Do you think that Örnólfur could be behind this terrible thing?'

'I feel there's more reason to suspect him than Markús. That's considering he argued furiously with Thorsteinn earlier that evening and called him a traitor.'

'A traitor? Is Dad supposed to have betrayed Örnólfur?'

'So it seems.'

'Betrayed him, how?'

'Your grandfather didn't hear anything more of the conversation. Or so he says.'

Rannveig tries to digest this new information.

'I don't understand it,' she says after a long silence. 'I saw Örnólfur greet Dad when he arrived at Skálholt, and they were just like normal.'

We each empty our glasses again.

'I need to check on my daughter,' I say, and get to my feet.

Rannveig follows me into her room.

Sóley Árdís is fast asleep.

I tuck the duvet in around her and switch off the light as I go back out into the corridor.

'Markús can't have children,' Rannveig says.

'He's infertile?'

'Yes. But he didn't know that when we got married.'

She sits back on the sofa.

I recharge the shot glasses with the Tennessee nectar.

'I was terribly disappointed at the time as I would love to have children,' she continues. 'But considering how things have turned out, maybe it's just as well.'

'He might well be innocent.'

'Yes, I still believe he is,' she replied with a deep sadness in her dark eyes. 'But Markús was unfaithful to me with my best friend. That changes everything between us.'

'Everything?'

'At first I was angry with Markús and jealous of Jónína,' she replies. 'But now I'm no longer angry or jealous, just deeply saddened.'

'Is that so?'

'It's the truth. A few days ago I was still in love with Markús, but now the love has disappeared, gone up in smoke, not that it's something I decided on. It just happened. Don't you think that's strange?'

'Love is in our genes, like any other hereditary illness,' I reply.

This makes Rannveig laugh for the first time this evening.

Thanks to Jack.

We chat in the living room until it's getting on for midnight.

Rannveig stumbles as she gets quickly to her feet.

I catch hold of her in my arms.

'Am I drunk?'

'Just about enough,' I reply.

We gaze into each other's eyes.

'Isn't it best that you stay the night?' I ask.

She nods.

I help her to the bedroom, where I help her out of her black outfit.

Rannveig pulls the duvet up to her neck.

She watches me undress.

I slip under the broad down duvet next to her. Naked.

She turns to me.

'Hold me,' she whispers.

I roll onto my side and wrap her in my arms.

I feel sparks of lust flash through my body as I hold Rannveig tight against me. But I take care to hold back.

After a while, Rannveig looks up.

There are tears in her eyes.

'I feel so strange,' she says.

'I'm not surprised.'

'I mean, I no longer have a living father, my best friend betrayed me and is dead, and I've lost my husband,' she continues. 'All these awful events that I've no control over have forced me to say goodbye to so much in my life that's important. Without knowing what comes next.'

'Life always finds new directions,' I say.

Rannveig closes her eyes.

'Will you show me how to forget sorrow tonight?' she whispers.

28

Monday 28th June 2010

When I come home from taking Sóley Árdís to nursery, Rannveig is still asleep.

I sit on the edge of the bed and gaze at her.

There's a peaceful look on her face.

A night's rest has sent her sorrow and worries packing. For the moment, at least, thanks to sleep and orgasms.

I played her fabulous body like a fine instrument far into the night. Drove her crazy with my fingers and lips. Lit a fire of passion until she let herself be tipped over the edge.

Glorious!

Rannveig opens her eyes. She sees me sitting there.

It takes her a moment to realise where she is. She flushes as the memories of the night come rushing up from the depths of her mind.

'God!' she yelps, both hands to her mouth.

I smile.

'Was I so terribly drunk?'

'Not at all,' I reply.

'But I'm not that way inclined,' she says awkwardly.

'You were last night.'

I stand up, and fetch a soft pink dressing gown from the wardrobe. I lay it on the duvet.

'The shower's over there,' I say.

Rannveig sits up in bed. Her hands fly up to cover her breasts when she realises she's naked.

'Then there'll be breakfast in the kitchen,' I add.

'I...'

She gets no further with what she meant to say.

Rannveig looks at me as if she doesn't know how to put her feelings into words.

'There's no rush.'

I head for the kitchen. Another ink-black espresso and I sit at the table. Time to check the day's headlines.

My eye stops at *News Blog*'s headline.

Prosecution withdrawn

According to Máki's article, the police have confirmed that the case against *News Blog* for illegal publication of official documents was withdrawn at the end of last week.

On the other hand, a police spokesman stated in an interview with *News Blog* that although the person who had brought the prosecution to begin with had withdrawn it, a decision on any further action remains with the police. So there is no certainty that the investigation has been closed.

Rögnvaldur Rögnvaldsson's decision has taken me by surprise.

Right now the only possible reason I can find for this unexpected about-face is that the old man has discovered it was his son who handed Máki the secret files about the spy in cabinet.

Who told him?

And when?

Maybe Thorsteinn told him? What was that final conversation about, late on the Saturday evening at Skálholt?

That's the conversation Rögnvaldur dismissed as being a personal matter. Could it have been about the secret co-operation between Thorsteinn and Máki?

That's the only sensible explanation I can think of for Rögnvaldur's decision to withdraw his prosecution.

But if Thorsteinn had admitted to his father just a few hours before his death that he was Máki's source, then that begs another and no less urgent question.

How did Rögnvaldur respond to his son's confession?

The thought makes me shudder. And I see the murders at Skálholt in a completely new light.

Unless it's a misleading signal?

Rannveig appears in the kitchen in her black dress.

'I'm going home,' she says.

'Have a coffee before you go.'

She hesitates. Then sits at the table.

'I should thank you,' she says after the first sip of coffee.

'My pleasure.'

'I mean, it feels like I'm finally about to emerge from this horrible nightmare.'

'That's good.'

I go with her to the stairs. By the door, I take her arm.

'Don't forget that you can call me at any time.'

She nods.

Lísa Björk is already in the office.

We go over tasks for the day ahead. Then I call Arnlaugur in Selfoss, who confirms that Rögnvaldur provided an addition to his statement. But he won't give me any information on what this new testimony is.

'Rögnvaldur told you about the furious argument between Thorsteinn and Örnólfur Indriðason, didn't he?'

'Why ask if you already know?'

'I feel it's important in this case that your whole focus shouldn't be on my client,' I say. 'There's every reason to have other suspects in the frame who were at Skálholt that night.'

'We will, of course, investigate reliable leads that point in other directions. We have a responsibility to do that.'

'When does Rannveig get her father's belongings back?'

'Everything at Skálholt that belonged to Thorsteinn and Jónína was impounded by forensics, and some of that will remain in our custody until the justice system has concluded the case.'

'Does that includes his briefcase?'

I hear papers rustle for quite some time.

'I have a list here of Thorsteinn's belongings and there's no briefcase listed.'

'That's odd.'

'Who says he had a briefcase with him at Skálholt?'

'His daughter Rannveig has a film clip from the seminar, and Thorsteinn can be clearly seen with a red-brown briefcase in his hand as he arrived at Skálholt.'

'It's not on the list,' Arnlaugur repeats.

'Then we can speculate that the briefcase is in the murderer's keeping?'

There's a long silence on the phone.

'I need a copy of this recording,' the policeman says at last.

'No problem. If that'll prompt you to start searching for the case. And the real killer.'

Afterwards I sit for a while in my comfortable black boss chair and run through the whole thing in my mind.

The missing briefcase has given me new hope.

Right from the word go, Máki has been adamant that their co-operation was the reason behind Thorsteinn's murder at Skálholt. He could well be right. That's if the old newshound's manuscript was in Thorsteinn's briefcase.

There's one thing that's clear.

If I can link the missing briefcase directly to the murders at Skálholt, then that should be reason for the judge to have serious doubts about my client's guilt.

But that'll only happen if the city's finest can track down the briefcase. Or if they can at least show who took it, or stole it, shortly before or after the murders were committed.

To be honest, I don't imagine they're likely to manage that.

There are some people who couldn't find their own arses with both hands, as Mother said.

29

Attack is always the best form of defence.

The city's finest still haven't spoken to Örnólfur Indriðason about his conversation at Skálholt with Thorsteinn Rögnvaldsson. That's assuming I heard the chief superintendent correctly.

So I'm going to get in first.

Örnólfur's in the phone book. He agrees to meet.

'I normally go home at lunchtime,' he says.

'From where?'

'I'm working at the University of Reykjavík until midday, and then I cycle home.'

He lives in a ground floor place on Lynghagi.

Örnólfur invites me into the kitchen. Age and use haven't been kind to the dark wood of the kitchen fittings.

'Coffee or tea?'

'Black coffee.'

He fiddles with the coffee machine.

'I'm told that you and Thorsteinn were childhood friends?'

'That's true. Thorsteinn and I were neighbours in Seltjarnarnes for years, until my parents moved here. We were at college together.'

'And in the Movement?'

Örnólfur pours hot coffee into cups.

'Those were the best and the worst years of my life,' he says.

'How were they the best?'

'We were a group of young people working together for a better society. We believed that we could change the world and we put everything into the struggle.'

'And the worst?'

'The disappointment.'

I give Örnólfur a questioning look as he takes a seat facing me across the kitchen table.

'First and foremost, failing to reach people,' he replies. 'Practically nobody listened to what we had to say. On top of that was the bitter enmity of the establishment who set the police on us more than a few times. The reality was that it was hopeless and we were far too young and innocent to understand that.'

'Innocent?'

'Yes. Innocent in a political sense. Otherwise we'd have

given up the struggle long before.'

'Do you see that time as wasted years?'

'No, not at all,' Örnólfur replies. 'I amassed experience that has been of benefit to me ever since. But not everyone was so fortunate.'

'Meaning what?'

'Some of us sacrificed too much for the struggle and for those around them, and never amounted to anything in life. Then there were others, such as Thorsteinn, whose father was at the very heart of the establishment. That certainly helped his son in his professional life.'

'Were you envious of Thorsteinn?'

'No. Far from it. I'm fully aware that we each have our own cross to bear, even those of us who are rolling in money.'

'Would you explain that?'

'I understand that it wasn't always easy for Thorsteinn to live up to his father's expectations. He was forced to do some things that were contrary to his nature, and that preyed heavily on his mind, especially during the last few years of his life. He had many regrets about his younger years.'

'I'm told that you called Thorsteinn a 'fucking traitor' shortly before his death.'

Örnólfur blanches.

'Who says that?'

'Is it true?'

He gets quickly to his feet. He paces the kitchen floor, deep in thought. Then he sits down and glares angrily at me.

'I see,' he says. 'You're serving Rögnvaldur Rögnvaldsson, just as Thorsteinn did.'

'I'm serving nobody but my client,' I reply.

'That must be Rögnvaldur,' he continues without listening to me. 'He was there in the corridor when I came out of Thorsteinn's room that evening.'

'Why did you call Thorsteinn a traitor?'

'Don't you know that as well?'

'I prefer to hear it first-hand.'

Örnólfur clenches his fists. Brings them down hard on the table. The coffee cups dance.

'Then speak to that bastard Rögnvaldur Rögnvaldsson. He knows better than anyone what Thorsteinn had to say to me.'

'Rögnvaldur wasn't present at your conversation.'

Örnólfur snorts.

'Really? He could've spied on that, like so much else.'

Örnólfur's a dark horse. He's clearly a man with a temper, even though you wouldn't see that by looking at him. Tempestuous and angry.

I try to strike while the iron's hot.

'Tell me about Thorsteinn's confession,' I suggest.

'That's not going to stay a secret much longer,' he says after a pause. 'Thorsteinn said he'd told some journalist about all the dirty tricks.'

'What dirty tricks?'

'He betrayed us!' Örnólfur yells. 'We fought for a decade for our ideals. We tried to challenge the establishment with protests and direct action but the police always knew in advance what we were planning, because Thorsteinn had tipped them off. Instead of being one of the comrades, he was their stooge the whole time, an agent provocateur.'

'You must have been very angry when you heard this confession.'

'Yes, I was angry. I'm still angry.'

'Angry enough to seek revenge?'

Örnólfur stares furiously for a while. Then he suddenly breaks into laughter.

'Now I see where you're going with this conversation,' says at last. 'You're searching for a murderer.'

'Have I found one?'

'No.'

Örnólfur gets to his feet.

'If it had occurred to me to murder anyone that night at Skálholt, then I'd have acted against the spider at the centre of the web, and it seems clear that he's still spinning his threads,' he says as he shows me to the door.

30

Wednesday 30th June 2010

Fat Raggi calls me just before lunch.

'That was a wild goose chase you sent us on,' he says.

'Meaning what?'

'Results came through from the US this morning,' Raggi replies. 'The arm you found up there on the Snæfellsnes glacier isn't Cussler's.'

'So he's out of the picture completely?'

'That's what it looks like.'

'And the ring?'

'We forwarded the American professor's email to the FBI and they promised to check if there's any truth to this.'

'So you're no closer to finding out who this is?'

'Nope. Looks like we're back at square one.'

I thank him for the information. Then I write a short email to Jerome Higgins in New York. I explain that his hunch that the lost American John Adam Cussler's bones lie up there on the glacier hasn't turned out to be correct.

At the same time, Raggi tries to palm me off with excuses for his colleagues' slow progress in the Julia MacKenzie case.

'They haven't refused to reopen the case,' he repeats.

'But haven't agreed, either?'

'No, but you have to understand, my dear Stella, that this takes time.'

'You know Julia's mother doesn't have long to live,' I tell him. 'What's happened so far?'

'The National Police Commissioner sent an officer up north to speak to the brothers at Gullinhamrar and their yard manager,' Raggi replies. 'The same officer had already spoken to your witness, Birkir Brynjólfsson, who supplied the signed testimony that a foreign woman on a motorcycle had visited Gullinhamrar in July 2001.'

'And what did Jósteinn and Geiri have to say?'

'Neither of them could understand Birkir's account.'

'Really?'

'That's it. Neither Alexander nor Jósteinn could recall such a visit. They both say that if it took place in the summer of 2001, they must both have been absent that day.'

'But Birkir recalled clearly that they were both present.'

'They both deny it.'

'Then they're lying.'

'We're down to one man's word against another's, and that makes things difficult,' Raggi says. 'Our specialists are examining the accounts of all these witnesses and their reliability. The police's decision will be based on their assessment.'

'When?'

'As quickly as possible.'

I call Lísa Björk into my office. I tell her about Raggi's call.

'We're going to have to put some pressure on these jobsworths,' I say.

'I'm still waiting for replies to requests for information from the ministries of education in Kosovo and Serbia,' she replies. 'I'll send them reminders.'

'We're going to have to make public our demand for a new investigation into Julia's disappearance,' I say. 'That's the most effective way to kick the system into gear.'

'I presume you'll be cautious about mentioning Birkir Brynjólfsson's testimony, considering it conflicts with the accounts of Jósteinn and Alexander?'

'I'm just going to mention to Máki that Birkir saw Julia and her motorcycle at Gullinhamrar in July 2001.'

'No names mentioned?'

'Exactly. But I can't prevent Máki finding out who owns the farm up there.'

'I see.'

'Which he'll do, of course. That's how he rolls.'

I reach for the keyboard. I write a short outline of Julia's disappearance and the search in the summer of 2001. To this I add part of Birkir's account about the motorcycle he tried out in the yard at Gullinhamrar. Then I put in a few words about the request to the National Commissioner of Police for a new investigation into Julia's disappearance. Then I call Máki. He's happy to put together a news item from all this.

I email him the information I've put together. With it goes the photo of Julia and Geiri from Gullinhamrar chatting up there at Askja.

Máki calls in the afternoon.

'The story's online,' he says.

I call up *News Blog* onto my screen. The headline jumps out at me.

**Stella Blómkvist demands a new investigation
into the fate of British girl who vanished after
visiting equestrian centre in 2001.**

He's used my text almost verbatim. But he's added information about Gullinhamrar and its owners. And the photo is there with the story.

'Good stuff,' I tell him.

'This is worth keeping an eye on, considering Jósteinn Sveinsson's involvement as one of the owners of the farm,' he says with a touch of excitement.

'Why the interest in Jósteinn?'

'He has powerful friends in the Progressive Party and he's made good use of his connections,' Máki says. 'There are also those who say he has a long string of misdeeds behind him in Kosovo.'

'Really?'

'Yep. And in the next few days I'll dig into that.'

After that I call Gregory George MacKenzie. I update him on the progress I've made so far, and urge him to have his lawyers in Britain apply pressure on the National Commissioner of Police's office in Iceland to agree to my demand for a fresh investigation.

MacKenzie wants to hear in detail about my efforts to find his niece. I tell him about Birkir Brynjólfsson's account – and the response from Alexander and from Jósteinn Sveinsson.

'Personally, I'm convinced that Birkir is telling the truth,' I say. 'That he met Julia on the day she dropped out of sight, regardless of what Alexander and Jósteinn have to say. That's why we have to put pressure on the police to investigate what happened to Julia after her visit to Gullinhamrar, where she went from there. That's if she did continue her journey.'

'I'll use every bit of influence I can bring to bear,' MacKenzie replies. 'The British ambassador in Reykjavík is a good friend and he's familiar with this matter.'

'Excellent.'

The day passes quickly, with one job following on the heels of the next.

Rannveig calls that evening.

'I meant to look only forward and work on my films, but the past keeps getting in the way,' she says.

'What's up now?'

'Dad's estate.'

'Aha.'

'My grandfather persuaded the District Commissioner to agree to a simple disposal of the estate's assets, since I'm the only heir,' Rannveig continues. 'I have to go to the Westman Islands to fetch all kinds of documents relating to Dad's finances and to sort out the house. But the police still have his keys.'

'Would you like me to speak to the District Commissioner in Selfoss about releasing his keys?'

'Yes, and I was wondering if you'd come with me?'

'To the Westman Islands?'

'Yes. Because of his health, my grandfather doesn't feel up to it. He has a heart problem, and I'm sure you know much better than I do what paperwork I need to hand over for the estate to be dealt with.'

'When?'

'Saturday?'

It's a relief to hear that Rannveig appears to be back to her old self after our memorable night-time adventure.

More than likely we'll have to stay overnight in the Islands. A night, or maybe two.

Hmmm!

Dreams cost nothing.

31

Saturday 3rd July 2010

The chief superintendent on the Selfoss force isn't happy with me.

'I've a good mind to have you charged with hindering the investigation into the murders at Skálholt,' Arnlaugur said when I called him yesterday. 'As a lawyer you must be aware that it's an offence to exert influence over a witness in a criminal investigation.'

'Which I haven't done.'

'We took Örnólfur Indriðason's statement the day before yesterday and that's not what he says. You'd better leave witnesses alone in future, or I'll take all the necessary measures.'

All the same, I managed to get him to agree to allow Rannveig to have Thorsteinn's keys so that she could get into her father's house in the Westman Islands.

'They'll be at reception, in an envelope with her name on it,' he said.

'Anything new in the search for Thorsteinn's briefcase?' I asked as the conversation came to an end.

'No. Not that I can tell you about,' Arnlaugur snorted before hanging up.

It turns out that retired jobsworths are no less pissed off with me these days.

I like that. It's an indicator that I'm on the right track.

Such as when Alfreð Sveinsson, the former chief superintendent on the Sauðárkrókur force, called to yell at me after Máki's story about Julia MacKenzie's visit to Gullinhamrar appeared on *News Blog*.

'How dare you leak this kind of one-sided information to the media when it's obvious that this boy's testimony is nothing but a fantasy?' he roared down the phone.

'I simply believe what Birkir told me,' I replied. 'He has no reason to lie to us.'

'Both Jósteinn and Alexander have denied there's any truth to the boy's testimony.'

'All the same, it's my assessment that Birkir's account is correct and truthful.'

'Even though two witnesses are adamant that the boy must

have got his recollections mixed up?'

'Firstly, it's established that Geiri invited Julia to Gullinhamrar. Secondly, it's clear that Birkir is a bike nerd. It's highly likely that he remembers clearly, considering he got to try out her motorcycle. The only thing that's particularly odd is that neither Alexander nor your half-brother Jósteinn will admit that Julia called there.'

'There's nothing odd about it, considering she was never at Gullinhamrar.'

'Did you investigate that at the time?'

'There was no reason for that back then, any more than there is now,' Alfreð answered. 'Apart from that, I can inform you that Jósteinn is preparing a legal case against *News Blog* for insinuating that he might have had a hand in this girl's disappearance.'

'That sounds like a bundle of fun,' I said.

'What do you mean?'

'I mean that a legal case that revolves around Jósteinn's reputation would give me and Máki ample opportunity to dig deep into his past, both here and in Kosovo.'

That brought Alfreð to a sudden halt.

'You're barking up the wrong tree,' he retorts sulkily.

'I'm looking for a new, impartial investigation into Julia's disappearance, that's all.'

'That boy's fantasies are no basis for that.'

'The National Commissioner of Police will decide on that, not you.'

The conversation ended right there.

It's early in the morning and I pack my pink suitcase with clothes and cosmetics, before waking Sóley Árdís.

Sunshine and a light breeze greet me outside in the parking lot, under a clear sky.

Rannveig has abandoned the black of mourning for jeans, a sleeveless white top and pale walking shoes.

'Wow. You look great,' I say.

She puts her case away in the silver steed's boot. She says hello to my daughter, who's in the child seat in the back, and takes a seat by my side.

We head off.

'How long did your father live in the Westman Islands?' I ask on the way east.

'Mum died in 2001 and Dad went to work in the Westman

Islands about a year after that,' Rannveig replies. 'By then my grandfather had moved up to Thingvallasveit and I was on the way to study at film school in Germany, so he wanted a change as well.'

'And he bought himself a place in Heimaey?'

'Yes, he got one of the old houses that wasn't flattened by ash, fire and brimstone in the eruption in 1973.'

The house is painted white, but the roof is black. There's a ground floor, a basement and an attic space with two gable windows. It's clad in corrugated iron.

'Downstairs there's a living room, kitchen, bathroom and a little room that Dad used as an office,' Rannveig says as the silver steed comes to a halt outside. 'Three bedrooms upstairs, two of which are very small, utility and storerooms in the basement.'

We leave the cases in the hall.

Sóley Árdís scrambles up and down the wooden staircase.

Thorsteinn's office is tidy. A computer screen, keyboard and a mouse are on the desk, and there are no piles of paperwork. Shelves are filled with folders, marked by year.

'Do you have a password for the computer?' I ask.

'No,' Rannveig replies. 'But Dad wrote down all his passwords in a little black notebook. It must be here somewhere.'

I take down the folder for the current year. Taking a seat in a comfortable chair, I start going through the documents.

Thorsteinn has filed all the bills, bank statements and receipts by date.

'It's all very well organised,' I say.

'Yes, Dad was always on top of everything.'

I look through the desk drawers as I search for the black notebook.

'There's nothing edible in the fridge,' Rannveig says. 'I'll go down to the shop to get something for dinner.'

'Me too!' Sóley Árdís chimes in.

'Sure, you can come too,' Rannveig says.

I continue rooting through drawers. There's no notebook to be seen.

Next, I take a look at the previous year's folder of documents. I quickly get a clear picture of Thorsteinn's finances.

Going by his 2009 tax declaration, he had significant assets. These include shares in fisheries and tech companies, plus a bunch of government bonds.

His overall assets at the end of 2009 exceeded his debts by

around 110 million krónur. That includes the house, valued at around thirty million.

As the sole heir, Rannveig should be on easy street financially. That's to say, if she isn't already.

I take a break from the paperwork and take a look upstairs.

Thorsteinn had been using the large bedroom. There's a double bed, with two single duvets. One's neat and straight. The other isn't. That tells me he'd slept alone for the last few nights before going to the mainland to die.

I hear Rannveig and my daughter returning, and hurry back down. Between us we stock the fridge. Then we make some coffee.

'We need to change the bedclothes,' Rannveig says. 'Dad must have clean bed linen in the cupboard in the bedroom.'

Sóley Árdís precedes us up the stairs.

She scuttles into one of the small bedrooms and sits on the bed.

'I want to sleep here,' she says.

'No problem,' Rannveig replies. 'Help me find you some bedclothes.'

When they've found clean linen, she helps my daughter make up the bed she has chosen, and then sets about stripping the sheets from her father's bed.

'We only need one bed, don't we?' she says with a smirk.

Tasty!

'That should do,' I smile back.

32

Sunday 4th July 2010

By dinner time I'd put together all of the paperwork relating to Thorsteinn Rögnvaldsson's finances needed to settle the estate. It was all in a box in the back of the silver steed.

So that gave us the evening to relax.

We cooked a lovely meal. We chatted. We played with Sóley Árdís. She seems to like Rannveig as much as I do.

'What will you do with this house?' I ask after dinner.

'I'll hold on to the house,' Rannveig replies. 'That's what Dad would've wanted.'

'What makes you think that?'

'Haven't you taken a look at the basement?'

I shake my head.

'Dad has a kind of museum down in the cellar. We can have a look later or tomorrow.'

Sóley Árdís does her best to stretch out the adventure. She keeps herself awake past midnight. Then she dozes off in the living room.

It's around half past midnight when I pick her up. I take her up the stairs, get her in her pyjamas and tuck in the duvet around her.

'You have a delightful child,' Rannveig says.

'No surprise considering her immaculate conception!'

'That seems unlikely,' she says with a smile.

Rannveig goes ahead of me to the bedroom.

'I feel like a kid playing with forbidden fire,' she says, looking at me with a serious expression on her face. 'I've never had such feelings before for a woman. Maybe I'm just freaking out like an idiot because of all the shocks of the last couple of weeks.'

'Or maybe not.'

'I want to sleep with you again, but without being drunk, so that I can figure out what's going on.'

'Come here.'

I pull her close. Kiss her. First softly, then with passion.

She returns my kisses eagerly.

Then I pull off her sleeveless top. I kiss her bare breasts. I unbuckle the belt of her shorts, then slip them slowly down her legs.

'Lie on the duvet,' I say, breathing hard.

She obeys.

I can't keep my lascivious eyes off her nakedness as I pull off my own clothes.

I sit at her side, lean forward and kiss her again.

Tonight, Rannveig is no less eager than I am.

She longs to receive and to give.

Afterwards I hold her in my arms under the duvet.

'I think I'd like to play with this fire a little longer and see where it takes us,' she whispers.

Her caresses wake me in the morning.

Nice!

We're just getting steamy when a yawning Sóley Árdís comes into the bedroom.

She's seen me before with women in my arms in bed, so she's not taken by surprise.

'*Hœ*, darling,' I say. 'Mum's just coming.'

My daughter looks at Rannveig, who lies with her cheek resting on my belly.

'Are you my new mummydaddy?' she asks.

Rannveig can't help laughing.

I sit up in bed, and kiss the top of her head.

'Looks like we'll have to pick this up in the next exciting episode,' I say.

An hour later we're dressed and breakfast is behind us.

Rannveig has a crossing booked to the mainland in the afternoon.

'I really want to find Dad's notebook before we leave,' she says thoughtfully.

'Could it have been in his briefcase?'

'I don't know. Where is it?'

'It's not here in his office. But he had a briefcase with him at Skálholt that hasn't been found yet. The Selfoss police say they're looking for it.'

We pack our bags. Time to get ready to travel home.

'I still need to show you the museum,' Rannveig says.

'Can I see it?' Sóley Árdís asks. 'Can I see it too?'

The wooden staircase creaks as we follow her down to the basement.

Down here there's a washing machine and a dryer. There are white shelves, most of them empty. A green garden hose hangs on a hook under a narrow window.

The door to the storeroom is locked. But Rannveig soon finds the right key.

Like everything else in Thorsteinn's house, everything in this windowless room is carefully organised.

There are light brown shelves on one wall. It looks to me like they're full of books, pamphlets and all kinds of remarkable items.

On the wall opposite, Thorsteinn has lined up frames of different sizes. In some are photographs, monochrome and colour, along with posters and leaflets of different kinds in others.

Further along, under the storeroom's far end facing the door, are a dark brown armchair and small coffee table.

'Dad said he'd collected all these things together so that he wouldn't forget his younger days,' Rannveig says. 'To begin with, he had all this museum stuff in boxes in the cellar at the house in Seltjarnarnes, but he took it all with him when he moved to the Westman Islands and hung everything up here.'

I look more closely at the pictures on the wall. Some are of long-dead people whose faces I recognise. Che is still famous. So is Mao.

Between the portraits are photographs of demonstrations and political battles fought in the streets, both here and abroad.

'You recognise any of these people?'

'That's Ho Chi Minh, who was President of Vietnam, and that's Allende who was overthrown in Chile,' Rannveig replies. 'Ulrike Meinhof is in there somewhere. You know, the German terrorist.'

'Did your father admire her?'

'When Dad was a young man, he was deeply involved in protests and got caught up in a few fights with the police. There are supposed to be pictures of him here somewhere protesting about the US military presence in Iceland.'

She shows me a row of pictures of young people with placards.

'That's Dad,' she says. 'The picture was taken the year Nixon came to Reykjavík to meet the President of France.'

Despite the full beard and his being thirty-seven years younger in the photo than the man in Rannveig's images of him, I recognise Thorsteinn immediately. He's one of a large group waving placards, demanding *Iceland out of NATO* and *US Army Out*.

'That's Örnólfur Indriðason there next to Dad. The others I don't know by name.'

I peer closer at the picture.

Örnólfur appears to have changed less over the years than Thorsteinn, probably because he still has a beard.

Thorsteinn, Örnólfur and a young man standing next to them are all holding their protest placards high, clearly yelling out a slogan.

'They look like they're having fun,' I say.

'Dad often spoke about those old days as if they were some wonderful adventure,' Rannveig replies. 'But he'd long stopped being a radical leftist. Mum sometimes teased him and said that he went whichever way the political wind blew.'

The colour image is remarkably clear. It's printed on excellent paper.

I make out the faces of five angry young men. There are seven if you count the two standing a little behind. They're chanting slogans nobody remembers these days, waving placards and clenched fists.

A clenched fist?

I look even more closely at the young man standing next to Örnólfur.

The lad grasps the handle holding up his placard, with a bunched fist directly pointing at the lens.

On one finger there's a large ring with a red stone – a large, square red stone.

33

Monday 5th July 2010

I'm on the way to the shores of Lake Thingvellir.

Rögnvaldur Rögnvaldsson has asked me to meet him. No preamble, no explanation, a man who's used to getting his own way.

He wouldn't say why he wanted to meet.

All the same, I accepted.

Pure curiosity drove my decision, as so often before.

The old guy has made himself comfortable in a magnificent house just above the shore of the lake. From the road his house can barely be seen for the trees that form a barrier on three sides.

The sign reads *Himinbjörg*.

There's a black 4x4 on the gravel track, by the entrance. There's a white and blue speedboat moored to a pontoon that juts a few metres into the lake.

Rögnvaldur sits in an easy chair at a table under the trees. He's dressed to keep warm, even though it's the height of a hot summer.

'Welcome,' he says in his hoarse voice. 'There's hot coffee in the flask, in case you're thirsty.'

I take a seat facing him, and pour hot coffee into a large cup.

It's surprisingly good.

'Why that name for the house?' I ask. 'You're already in heaven?'

'Himinbjörg was the dwelling of Heimdall, the messenger of the Norse gods.'

'And?'

'For a long time, my duties were much the same as those of Heimdall.'

'Which were?'

'His role was to spy on the intentions of the enemies of the gods.'

'Aha.'

'There are two reasons for asking you to come here, for a chat and for some advice,' Rögnvaldur continues.

'Which comes first?'

'I'm an old man and can't be sure of many remaining good years.'

'Nobody escapes death for ever. And the second reason?'

'The unexpected death of my son Thorsteinn.'

Rögnvaldur reaches for a plastic folder lying on the grass beside him, and places two sheet of paper on the table.

'I want to make use of your legal services,' he says. 'Here's your contract, in duplicate.'

'But you're a lawyer yourself.'

'That's of little use once I'm incapacitated or dead.'

'Why me?'

'Rannveig trusts you,' he replies. 'She's my only living descendant and, as such, I must take her wishes into consideration.'

'Is she aware of this meeting?'

'She is.'

I sip the black coffee.

'In all honesty, I'd have many weighty reasons to avoid you like the plague,' he continues.

'And what are those reasons?'

'Your actions in recent years in general indicate that you are by nature an anarchist and you despise civilised society.'

'Really?'

'I feel it's a glaring example of your cracked morality that you as a lawyer should seduce your client's wife.'

'I'm simply trying to comfort Rannveig,' I snap back. 'She needs all the support she can get.'

'Rannveig's future is much on my mind, as she's the last of our line. My family will die out if she doesn't have a child. That mustn't happen.'

'Markús isn't going to help much in that respect. That's even if I can get him released.'

'I know he's impotent.' Rögnvaldur coughs, then puts emphasis on every word. 'Rannveig listens to you. You must encourage her to divorce him.'

'Isn't that up to her?'

Rögnvaldur leans forward.

'Sign the contract,' he says. 'Otherwise we cannot speak in confidence.'

It doesn't take long to read through it. It's short and to the point.

'If you have any testimony to make that could benefit Markús Hálfdánarson, then I can't sign an agreement that requires me to keep quiet.'

'I can assure you that nothing I have to say about that foul incident will strengthen Markús's case.'

'In that case I want to add that as a condition of this agreement.'

'Agreed.'

'I also act for Máki, the editor of *News Blog*.'

'That's why I withdrew my legal action against the journalist. I am no longer involved with that prosecution. So that removes any conflict of interest.'

'You seem to have thought of everything.'

'It's an old habit.'

I sign both copies, having added the codicil. He does the same.

Then I take one copy, fold it in two and stow it in a pocket of my russet-brown leather jacket.

'Let's move into the house,' Rögnvaldur says, and he shows me into a magnificent living room. The furniture is all old and classy. Tables and fittings are solid oak. The sofa and two armchairs are upholstered in dark leather. Large paintings in gilded frames hang on the walls.

We sit in the deep armchairs.

'While Thorsteinn was alive, I could avoid facing the realities of approaching death,' he says. 'He knew most of the secrets of my life, but that's not the case with Rannveig. She knows little or nothing of my life's work and is not prepared to assess what should be done when I'm gone.'

'But even Thorsteinn turned his back on you, didn't he?'

'I'm accustomed to betrayal,' Rögnvaldur replies. 'I stood for decades on the front line. But when the Cold War ended, nobody wanted to acknowledge the heroism of our actions. Even the Americans, whom we and other true Icelanders supported through thick and thin with countless actions behind the scenes, turned their backs on us without even a word of thanks for the sacrifices we made on their behalf. But I must admit that the most hurtful thing of all was when Thorsteinn betrayed me. I never expected that.'

'He told you about his co-operation with Máki when you spoke for the last time at Skálholt?'

'You are sharp, as I was aware,' Rögnvaldur says. 'A few hours before he departed this world, Thorsteinn and I had a long and emotional conversation. He admitted that he had removed documents from my personal files and shown them to the *News*

Blog journalist. His confession took me completely by surprise. It had never occurred to me that Thorsteinn could ever betray my longstanding trust.'

'You were angry?'

'No. Not angry. More astonished and hurt. He tried to justify his betrayal of me as a necessary atonement for his betrayal of his comrades in the Movement in the past. We discussed all this, until he accepted that new betrayals do not redress old ones.'

'How did your conversation end?'

'Thorsteinn agreed to withdraw his co-operation with the journalist.'

'Even though they'd almost completed writing a book together?'

'He promised to withdraw everything he'd told the journalist.'

'I understand that Thorsteinn had the manuscript with him in his briefcase?'

'He showed me the manuscript,' Rögnvaldur replies. 'Naturally, I had no time to read it, but a quick examination of just a few pages confirmed its nature.'

'Where's the manuscript now?'

'It was on his bed when I left him.'

I look the old guy up and down.

'I find such willingness on his part to be highly unlikely. Your son betrayed you, and suddenly performs a *volte face* and you immediately forgive him. That sounds like the script of a TV soap opera. Are you telling me that you were reconciled when you parted?'

'We were as close to becoming as reconciled as was possible at that moment. My son had lost his way, then saw a light in the darkness and found his way home. He was willing to continue to keep my secrets after I depart this world. Thorsteinn's death is therefore not just a colossal emotional blow, but also an irredeemable loss and the reason why I have no choice but to trust and take you into my confidence, even if this is contrary to my own instincts.'

'Your lamentations remind me of Shakespeare's old king.'

'King Lear?' Rögnvaldur asks. 'Yes, his bitter end has come to mind recently, but I know my mental strength and endurance are greater than his.'

Self-deception is old age's dearest friend, as Mother said.

34

I still haven't figured out what Rögnvaldur Rögnvaldsson has in mind, or what exactly he wants from me.

But it doesn't cost anything to continue listening. If I don't like it, I can simply say no when we get to that point.

'Máki reckons you have more secrets filed away than anyone else in Iceland,' I say with a grin.

'I was more courageous than some of my colleagues,' Rögnvaldur replies. 'One of my former superiors was so terrified of exposure that he took secret files from the police in Reykjavík up to his summer cottage and burned them all in an old oil drum.'

'Didn't that make you nervous?'

'Everything relating to my forty-year struggle with the communists is still preserved in my files. The oldest documents are from 1952 when I first assisted the authorities in exposing and isolating Icelandic communists. The latest ones are from 1990 when the Soviet Union was falling apart. Those files represent the secret, hard and successful struggle of true Icelanders who were determined to preserve the nation and its people, and I wish to make arrangements so that the future of this archive is preserved when I'm gone.'

'How?'

'There are clear and unequivocal instructions in my will concerning the archive stored here, its preservation and use. I've already informed Rannveig of my plans and I expect nothing other than that she will respect my wishes.'

'So what's the problem?'

'Rannveig has neither the imagination nor the experience to stand guard over this memorial to my life's work,' he replies. 'She needs someone at her side who can ensure that the requirements of the will are followed precisely. As a lawyer and Rannveig's friend, you meet all the criteria.'

I stare at the old man.

'How on earth do you imagine that I would take on such a task for you?'

'I'm fully aware that you regard me as a tool of the establishment and a political dinosaur,' Rögnvaldur says. 'But bear in mind that you won't be doing this for me, as I'll be dead. This is a task to be carried out for Rannveig.'

'You know how to play on people's emotions.'

A tired smile crosses his face. He's played his biggest trump card.

'Is this archive supposed to be open to the public, or locked away for years to come?'

'These days most people prefer to forget what we had to do to ensure the freedom of Icelanders during the Cold War, and forget those who took part in the war on communism,' he replies. 'Vision and lofty aims are all about money and nothing else. There's no understanding today of the exploits of those of us who gambled everything for the nation. But that will change. The time will come when the country will value our contribution for what it's really worth, and then my archive will be an invaluable source of insight for historians and politicians wishing to learn from the past.'

'Are you going to show me the big secret?'

'If you take on this role. Otherwise not.'

'It looks like I have nothing to lose.'

Rögnvaldur hands me a copy of his will.

It's a document on three sheets of paper. I see he's already included my name and role in it. Not that he asked me first.

Arrogant bastard.

I sign the agreement that's attached to the will. This sets out my duties to be carried out on his death, or in the event of Rögnvaldur becoming incapacitated for health reasons, unable to attend to his own affairs.

'My chief fear has been, and still is, that the brain fails before the heart,' he says.

There's a cellar beneath the house. There's no sign of it from outside the building.

Rögnvaldur goes ahead of me into a small room in which books fill shelves on almost the whole wall space. He takes a little remote control that lies on the desk and aims it at a cabinet in the corner.

I hear a low click.

Rögnvaldur goes to the cabinet and turns it to one side.

This exposes concrete steps leading down to the basement. At the foot of these is a steel fire door with a combination lock.

Rögnvaldur punches buttons on the lock, opens the door and steps into the space beyond.

There are grey filing cabinets that fill most of the floor. They're marked in alphabetical order, from A to Ö.

I go over to one and pull a drawer open. It's packed with

dark blue folders, each marked with a person's name.

I'm shocked at the sight of all this.

'How many personal dossiers are here?' I ask.

'I lost count of them back in the seventies,' Rögnvaldur replies.

'These people could hardly all have been dangerous communists?'

'Many people were infected by the communist virus without admitting it to themselves or to others. I can assure you that the majority of those whose records are here were at the time considered to be dangerous to the freedom and independence of our country. It was our duty to monitor them to ensure that they didn't cause serious damage.'

There's no hiding the fact that Rögnvaldur is proud of his archive. And that applies to more than just the paperwork.

'This archive is a genuine technical marvel,' he says.

'How so?'

'A special computer controls everything in here, including temperature, humidity and oxygen levels, to ensure that the files are stored under the best possible conditions. The computer is also programmed to react if a fire were to break out. It will lock the archive instantly, stopping the flow of oxygen and extinguishing the fire. I bought only the best.'

Shortly afterwards we're back in the armchairs in the living room.

'Why wait so many years without being certain of the country's reaction to this information?' I ask.

'What do you mean?'

'The archive has its own significant historical value, but you're the only man who knows the whole story.'

'The only one still living.'

'Why not tell the story yourself? Instead of leaving it to the historians of the future to interpret all this information as they see fit?'

'I have neither the talent nor the time to put my story on paper.'

'It should be easy enough to find a historian to work on it with you. Or a journalist.'

'Hacks are only interested in trivia.'

'This could take the form of an interview about your forty-year career and your sacrifices. Your story in your own words.

Aren't you accustomed to steering conversations the way you want them to go?'

Rögnvaldur meditates for a moment.

'Sometimes you have to raise your own monument, instead of waiting endlessly for others to do it,' I add.

The idea has clearly taken him by surprise.

I can see an internal struggle going on in Rögnvaldur's thoughts. On one side is his loathing of journalists. Against this is pitted his longstanding determination for his undervalued life's work to be recognised.

Which will win the day?

The glitter of fame teases the mind like a mirage in the desert, as Mother said.

35

Wednesday 7th July 2010

Sheesh!

I can't get it out of my mind, that square red stone on that lad's finger in the picture of the Movement comrades protesting against NATO and the military presence.

More than likely it's a complete coincidence that the boy wore a ring that resembled the Loki Fellowship members' ring. No doubt there are plenty of rings similar to the one I found on that deep-frozen hand up on the Snæfellsnes glacier – but without the letter L beneath the stone.

All the same, I brought the photo from Thorsteinn's museum back to town with me.

What for?

Well, because if anyone's going to remember the ring belonging to that lad, it's going to be the man standing next to him. That's Örnólfur Indriðason.

He should at least be able to give me the boy's name. That way I can track him down. I might get to see the ring for myself, remove all doubt.

Most likely this is just me setting out on a wild goose chase.

But this kind of wild goose chase won't leave me alone. I started taking hunches like this one seriously quite some time ago.

I call Örnólfur. He's on the way to a class. The last thing he wants to do is talk to me.

'The police in Selfoss warned me about you,' he says.

'I'm not going to ask you about the murders at Skálholt.'

'Then what?'

'I want to show you a picture of a demonstration you took part in, in the spring of 1973.'

'What on earth is your interest in that protest march?'

'Meet me later and I'll tell you.'

The old guy hesitates.

But he gives in to his own curiosity. He agrees to meet in the canteen at the University of Reykjavík at midday.

He's ploughing through mince and spaghetti when I turn up.

I take a seat next to him and take the photo from my russet-brown briefcase.

Örnólfur puts aside his knife and fork on the plate.
He holds the framed picture in both hands. He nods.
'I remember this demo,' he says.
'Great.'
'It was the day Nixon and Pompidou met at Kjarvalsstaðir,'
he continues. 'We took the opportunity to protest against the US
military presence and demanded that Iceland leave NATO.'
'Who's that next to you?'
'That's Thorsteinn. He had a proper beard back in those
days.'
'Can you identify any others?'
'That's Ófeigur next to Thorsteinn and Símon behind him.'
'Who's Ófeigur?'
'Ófeigur Gunnarsson. We were at college together. He
went abroad to study art and became a teacher when he returned
home. I lost all contact with Ófeigur, and then he rang me up this
summer and we met at Skálholt.'
'Was he present at the seminar?'
Örnólfur nods.
'And what about this Símon?'
'He became a lawyer. Símon Andrésson.'
I peer closely at the picture.
'Is that Símon Andrésson who's now a departmental head at
the Ministry of Justice?'
'Yes. He and Thorsteinn were very close at that time.'
I'd never have recognised the man in the picture. He's
changed so much.
'And who's that on your left?'
Örnólfur doesn't reply right away. He stares at the picture
with a look of sorrow.
'It's a long time since I last saw a picture of Gunnsteinn,'
he says at last.
'This lad's name is Gunnsteinn?'
'Gunnsteinn Ástráðsson.'
'Any idea where he is now?'
Örnólfur's eyes don't leave the photo.
'I need to speak to him,' I add.
'What for?'
'You see the ring he's wearing? I need to take a look at it.'
'The ring?'
'Yes. You remember seeing it?'
Örnólfur sighs.

133

'I recall Gunnsteinn being very proud of that ring,' he says.
'Do you know where he got it from?'
'There was some tale behind it.'
'Meaning what?'
'Gunnsteinn had a greater talent than most of us for turning something banal and everyday into an adventure, because he was a born misunderstood artist.'
'You remember the tale?'
'He met some American at Hotel Loftleiðir.'
'And?'
'When he came back, he had that ring.'
'Back where?'
'He rented a room from us.'
'On Lynghagi?'
Örnólfur nods.
'He bought the ring from this American?'
'Bought it, stole it, or was paid with it.'
'Paid for what?'
'Gunnsteinn was always broke,' Örnólfur replies. 'He made some extra cash by meeting foreigners at Hótel Loftleiðir or Hótel Saga.'
'For what?'
'What do you think?' he snaps.
Aha!
'It wasn't easy being a homosexual in Iceland at that time,' Örnólfur adds. 'Gunnsteinn had a hell of a tough time of it, poor lad.'
'Any idea of the name of this American who gave Gunnsteinn the ring?'
'No.'
I digest this new information for a moment.
'And you've no idea where Gunnsteinn is now?'
'No. Nobody knows.'
'Nobody? What do you mean?'
'Most people believed he was going to take the ferry across to Akranes, and then he ended up in the sea. But that was just gossip.'
Wow!
'You're telling me Gunnsteinn disappeared?'
'The search didn't find anything.'
'When did this happen?'
Örnólfur looks down at the picture again.

'He vanished that same spring,' he says. 'It was the spring of 1973.'

'Where was his family?'

'Gunnsteinn had a younger sister who lived in Raufarhöfn. A couple of times she came to visit him at Lynghagi.'

I slip the photo back in my briefcase.

'Was there anything special about the ring?' I ask.

'I recall that the red stone was beautiful.'

'Did you see anything under the stone?'

'Such as what?'

'A letter, or anything like that?'

'Not that I remember.'

'And you believe that Gunnsteinn received the ring for going to bed with this American?'

Örnólfur looks up.

'I always suspected that he stole it,' he replies.

'Why's that?'

'Gunnsteinn had no qualms when it came to drunk foreigners who were his customers. And I always felt that the ring was too valuable to be payment for a quick fuck.'

'I see.'

'But that wasn't what he claimed.'

Back at the office, I search online for newspapers from the summer of 1973. I find a few short articles about Gunnsteinn's disappearance, which didn't seem to have attracted much attention. That's most likely because he was believed to have fallen into the sea on the ferry crossing to Akranes.

The sea often takes a long time to return what it's taken. But it does eventually. As do the glaciers.

36

Friday 9th July

Rannveig has set off on another filming session for her glacier series. This weekend she'll be up on Langjökull with Pálmi and Jón Pétur – and a well-known lady novelist.

Sheesh!

I'm missing her far too much. I'm like a lovesick teen. You wouldn't imagine she's had enough of playing with forbidden fire.

My love affairs have never lasted long. Except for Ludmilla, the stunner from Latvia. But there's every chance that was because she spent most of every year abroad.

That afternoon Máki publishes a detailed report on *News Blog* of the police investigation at Skálholt. He places plenty of emphasis on the fact that one of the two victims at Thorláksbúð had argued furiously with another of the seminar participants shortly before his murder. That's someone other than Markús Hálfdánarson, who's currently on remand, suspected of the murders.

The information came from me. That goes without saying. And he agreed to my request to leave Örnólfur Indriðason's name out of it, for the moment.

The news item is intended to raise doubts about my client's guilt. And to help soften Rannveig's pain.

It doesn't take Raggi long to figure out my strategy. He's a smart guy.

'You're no more reluctant than usual to manipulate the media,' he says with a grin as I make myself comfortable in his office.

'I'm not the only one who's good at leaking information,' I shoot back.

'Arnlaugur over in Selfoss was complaining about you the other day. I told him to stand on his own two feet and not give way.'

'Am I supposed to take that as a threat?'

'He has a long fuse. But if you cross the line too many times, you can expect him to hit back hard.'

'You know I enjoy a fight.'

'Yeah. Tell me about it.'

Raggi has no fresh news of the efforts of the city's finest to put a name to the human remains found on Snæfellsnes glacier.

'Fingerprint comparison hasn't taken us anywhere so far,' he says.

'I have something new for you.'

'That last pointer you gave me made us look like idiots,' Raggi says with a scowl. 'Our colleagues in the US pissed themselves laughing at us being so gullible. They thought it was hilarious that the Icelandic police imagined that one of their former secret service chiefs could be under the ice of an Icelandic glacier.'

I hand Raggi my notes about Gunnsteinn Ástráðsson, in which I quote Örnólfur Indriðason's testimony concerning the ring that's visible on Gunnsteinn's finger in the picture of the anti-NATO demonstration in the spring of 1973. With it is a high-quality copy of the photo.

Raggi reads my notes and peers at the photo.

'So we're supposed to investigate every man who has a ring with a red stone?' he asks drily.

'Gunnsteinn's sister's name is Hallbera,' I add without rising to Raggi's bait. 'She's alive and lives in Raufarhöfn. I'd suggest comparing DNA samples from Hallbera and the frozen arm. It's no big deal, and it might solve the mystery.'

'DNA analysis costs money.'

'Well, if the DNA analysis shows that the arm is her brother's, then you don't need to spend more on fingerprint comparisons all over the world.'

'To be honest, we're fed up with your April Fool's pranks in the middle of summer,' he says.

'I wouldn't dream of telling you how to do your jobs, even though I was the one who stumbled across the arm on the glacier,' I reply.

Raggi sighs.

'I ought to mention that I haven't been in touch with Hallbera. If you don't act on this information, then of course I'll contact her and ask if she feels this is a realistic possibility.'

'Will you now?'

'I'm sure that Hallbera has always wondered what became of her brother and will see this new information as an unexpected opportunity to explain his disappearance,' I continue. 'In which case you'll no doubt hear from her yourself. Either in person or via the media.'

'You don't take no for an answer, do you, Stella?' Raggi says heavily.

'Up to you, Raggi.'

I get to my feet. I turn in the doorway.

'Apart from that, is there a decision yet on the Julia MacKenzie investigation?'

Raggi shifts in his chair.

'There is,' he replies.

'So is the investigation in progress?'

'I understand that the National Commissioner has come to the conclusion that there are no grounds for instigating a new investigation into her disappearance,' he replies. 'You'll be getting written confirmation in the next few days.'

'I don't believe this!'

'No doubt the National Commissioner has considered the matter with all due care.'

'Fucking bullshit,' I snap back. 'He just doesn't want to admit that the cops screwed up the investigation back in 2001.'

'You're welcome to your opinion. But it's not the position of the force that the investigation at the time was conducted wrongly.'

I glare furiously at Raggi.

The chief superintendent quickly avoids my furious stare.

'A bunch of fucking jobsworths,' I yell. 'You never change!'

I slam the door behind me.

37

Wednesday 14th July 2010

I pull up in the yard at Litla Hraun.

This visit is to inform Markús Hálfdánarson of the outcome of the autopsies carried out on the bodies of Thorsteinn Rögnvaldsson and Jónína Katrín Nönnudóttir.

'The conclusions confirm the pathologist's initial findings concerning the cause of death,' I tell him. 'There were no indications of defensive injuries, which supports the assumption that the assault took them completely unawares. The specialists also agree that the fire in Thorláksbúð was started by a candle or candles burning on the floor.'

Markús is due another appearance before the judge on Friday. That's the day his remand order ends.

The chief superintendent at Selfoss informed me this morning that they will be requesting a four-week extension of his remand.

'He's still the only one we have reason to suspect for this,' Arnlaugur said. 'It doesn't matter how much information you leak to the press, that hasn't changed.'

'I can't help wondering how you can see when your eyes are shut?' I ask sharply.

During our conversation, Markús remains remarkably calm.

'Are you doped up?' I ask.

'Yes. The doctor gave me something to calm me down,' he replies. 'He gave me sleeping pills as well. Otherwise I can't sleep in this place.'

Markús has nothing to add to help his own defence.

He just repeatedly protests his innocence. He repeats that he loves Rannveig, despite the two-year affair with Jónína Katrín. He asks how she is.

'She's busy with those glacier films,' I reply.

'Work often helps suppress bad thoughts,' he says. 'I find one of the worst things about prison is being idle all day long. That's especially because I have far too much time here to think over all the mistakes I've made in life, and it's driving me crazy. That's why I needed tranquillisers.'

Arnlaugur mentioned this morning that he sees no reason to question my client again in the near future.

'Not unless he's ready to confess,' he added.

'Markús is sticking to his testimony and is adamant he's innocent,' I replied.

'Then we'll let the evidence speak for itself.'

'Pretty thin evidence.'

'We consider it's enough to secure a conviction.'

Once I'm finished at Litla Hraun, I call Rannveig.

She's back home in Seltjarnarnes after the trip to Langjökull. She invites me round.

I put my foot down, heading back to the city in the silver steed.

Rannveig looks great. She's in black trousers and a pale sweater.

She listens with interest to my account of the conversations with Markús and Arnlaugur that morning, while we have a light lunch in her tasteful kitchen.

'Is there any chance he could be freed on Friday?' she asks.

'Judges normally tend to go along with police requests for remand,' I reply. 'But I'll do my best to get him released.'

'Is Markús innocent?'

'Are you starting to have doubts?'

'I just feel I need to be prepared for the possibility that he might have done it.'

'As his defence lawyer, I work on the premise that he's innocent. But, unfortunately, I don't know who murdered your father and Jónína.'

Rannveig takes a cup of coffee with her to the studio where she's working on the footage recorded on Langjökull.

'It went pretty well,' she says with a smile, sitting in front of the computer. 'But not as well as up on the Snæfellsnes glacier, as nobody fell into any crevasses and we didn't find any bodies up there.'

It gladdens my heart to see her laugh.

I sit beside her. For a while we watch some of the cool sequences recorded on the glacier. None of this does anything to alter my promise to myself to never set foot on a glacier ever again.

Finally, I push aside the long, dark hair from her cheek. I put a gentle hand on the back of her neck. Slowly but surely, I pull her to me.

Rannveig passionately returns my kisses.

'Come on,' she pants. She leads me to the bedroom.

Wonderful!

Back at the office around three in the afternoon, there's a stack of jobs to be dealt with. Even though my mind's elsewhere, still in Rannveig's arms.

Raggi calls just as I'm about to fetch my daughter from nursery. Sometimes this cop's my friend.

'Cooled down?' he asks cautiously.

I reply with a question of my own.

'Do you have any better news for me than last time we spoke?'

'We've been in touch with Hallbera Ástráðsdóttir and she has agreed to provide us with genetic samples,' Raggi says. 'It could take a few weeks to get a conclusion, but we'll try and speed things up.'

'Of course, I'm aware that I was giving you grief for the decisions of others,' I say.

'And I understand your disappointment,' he replies.

That's where we leave things.

Neither of us is any good at apologies.

Sometimes it's easier to climb Everest than to say sorry, as Mother said.

38

Friday 16th July 2010

Jósteinn's Sveinsson's threats have zero effect on Máki.

This morning he's cheerfully published an article on *News Blog* about the profitable aid provided by Iceland in Kosovo after the Albanian majority decided to leave Serbia and persuaded NATO to bomb the Serbs into acquiescence. The headline hits the bullseye.

Icelanders strike it rich in Kosovo

Máki lays out the background of the Albanian majority in Kosovo with blood on its hands becoming all-powerful in the wake of the bombings. This was followed by NATO and the European Union competing to keep alive this tiny state that had previously been part of Serbia, and before that, the former Yugoslavia that had splintered into a handful of states during the nineties.

When the Serbs had given up, it fell to the Icelandic state to manage the construction and subsequently the privatisation of the airport in Pristina, the capital of Kosovo, all of which yielded a healthy return for a limited company under the ownership of the Icelandic state.

He quotes a report in Swedish newspaper *Dagens Nyheter* in which one of the United Nations staff accused Icelanders of 'stealing the airport.'

'Among the air traffic controllers who travelled year after year to Kosovo as part of this programme was Jósteinn Sveinsson, the owner of the farm at Gullinhamrar in Skagafjörður, which has been recently in the news because of the disappearance there nine years ago of a young British woman,' Máki writes.

He doesn't stop there and continues with an account of Angjelo Skender Gjergji, brought by Jósteinn to Iceland to work at Gullinhamrar. He points out the remarkable speed with which Gjergji was able to obtain Icelandic citizenship and become Alexander – and adds that he has since regularly travelled as an Icelandic citizen to Kosovo with Jósteinn, without any apparent reason for accompanying him.

Máki expands on the iron grip that criminal gangs have on

business and politics in Kosovo, and the allegations of close links between gangsters and the former Albanian separatist fighters who have run the place for decades under the protective wing of the European Union, without bothering to clean up local politics or dealing with criminal gangs.

The old newshound is careful to make no allegations about any possible links between Jósteinn and Alexander with the Albanian mafia in Kosovo. But he leaves it to the reader to see what lies between the lines – and to speculate about how the man became as wealthy as he is now.

Máki is cheerful when I speak to him in the afternoon.

'Jósteinn should have the sense not to threaten me,' he says.

'Have you heard from him since the article was published?'

'I had an email from his lawyer with an observation that I'm looking into,' Máki says. 'But he hasn't sued me.'

Markús Hálfdánarson is due before the district judge at two.

I get to meet him in the courtroom ten minutes before the hearing.

He's just as relaxed as he was before. All the same, something in his attitude has changed since I met him at Litla Hraun a week ago.

'How's it going?' he asks.

'We'll see.'

'What are the chances?'

'This judge makes a habit of doing what the cops ask for.'

'So I could be inside for another month?'

'That wouldn't come as a surprise.'

'If that's the case, then I need to speak to you before they take me back to prison,' he says, a frown of concentration on his face.

'Are you considering changing your evidence?'

'I don't want to discuss it until the judge has done his stuff.'

There's no way of knowing what Markús has in mind.

Surely he's not going to confess to the murders at Thorláksbúð?

The representative of the Selfoss District Commissioner requests a four-week extension to Markús's remand. His justification for this is that the police have important aspects of the case that still need to be concluded. These include obtaining results of the DNA samples from the golf club.

I object to the District Commissioner's demand. I remind

the judge that the entire police case is based on conjecture and guesswork, that the police don't have a single witness who observed Markús Hálfdánarson at Thorláksbúð on the night the murders were committed. Neither have they produced any evidence to prove that he was there. On top of that, the police haven't even been able to track down the briefcase that Thorsteinn Rögnvaldsson definitely had with him at Skálholt.

'There's a strong likelihood that the contents of that briefcase were the real reasons behind the murders at Thorláksbúð,' I say. 'This indicates that someone other than my client committed this crime, and he has consistently protested his innocence the whole time. It's unjust and a serious contravention of Markús Hálfdánarson's human rights to deprive him of his liberty and to keep him in isolation for months on the basis of such flimsy reasoning.'

The judge asks the District Commissioner's representative a few questions about progress being made on the case. But his chief point of interest is when the DNA results can be expected, and what has been done to find Thorsteinn's briefcase.

Then he calls a pause in proceedings to consider.

'Isn't taking time to think it over positive?' Markús whispers.

'He didn't do it last time.'

'Exactly.'

When the hearing resumes after a half-hour break, the judge has taken the wisdom of Solomon on board. He's chosen to extend my client's remand by two weeks. That's half the time the boys in black claimed they needed.

The outcome leaves Markús thoughtful.

'I would see this hesitation on the part of the judge as being favourable for the next steps,' I tell him.

'True,' he says. 'But even two weeks pass very slowly in prison. Taking that into consideration, I'll wait a little longer. I can't sacrifice myself endlessly for other people.'

I'm startled.

'What do you mean?'

'Just what I said.'

I stare at my client as the city's finest lead him from the courtroom. Now the question spinning at light speed in my head is a simple one.

For whom is Markús sacrificing himself?

Heading home in the silver steed, I absolutely refuse to believe the answer to this question that seems to be the most obvious one.

39

Monday 19th July 2010

I'm awake early in the morning.

The persistent question from last Friday pops up right away in my mind.

For whom is Markús Hálfdánarson prepared to sacrifice himself? Temporarily, at least?

Presumably for Rannveig. Possibly also for her grandfather.

Or for Jónína Katrín, his lover.

But she's dead, and therefore out of the picture.

Rannveig and Rögnvaldur?

There's nobody else who fits the bill.

Sitting at my laptop, I again go through the Selfoss police force's report. I need to get a clearer picture of the timeline of events that terrible night at Skálholt.

Who was where, and when?

The pathologist estimates the time of death as after two in the morning. Where was Markús Hálfdánarson at that time?

My client admitted immediately that he'd been out in the yard at Skálholt between eleven and midnight. He chatted to several of the seminar guests outside in the fine weather. That was before he and his wife went back inside.

Rannveig fell asleep around midnight. But Markús was restless. He got up and went to his lover's room. But Jónína wasn't there.

That was around half-past midnight. So he says.

Markús had initially told us that he'd gone straight back to Rannveig. But a witness saw him outside at around one-thirty. That's between half an hour to an hour before Thorsteinn and Jónína were murdered.

That means my client lied to me and to the boys in black. He was outside in the yard at Skálholt shortly before the murders were committed.

Once a liar, always a liar?

I've no idea if that applies in this instance. But it always pays to be cautious.

I get back to the morning routine. Time to get Sóley Árdís up and dressed. Then it's breakfast. After that I take her to nursery.

When I get back there's a message from the prison at Litla Hraun.

I call the chief warder, who tells me that my client has requested a meeting with me at the earliest opportunity. So I head out east.

Markús is a bundle of nerves.

'I can't take being here much longer,' he says.

'Didn't you see the doctor this morning?'

'He just tells me to take the tablets, and I do. But they're less and less effective as time goes on.'

'What do you want to tell me?'

'I've tried to protect the family. But I can't any longer.'

'What do you mean?'

'You know I said I went outside around one-thirty that night?' he replies.

'Yes. A witness saw you outside at that time.'

'I went outside for a smoke. Just before I finished my cigarette, I saw Rannveig and Rögnvaldur walking from the church.'

'The Skálholt church?'

'Yes.'

'When was this?'

'It must have been round about a quarter to two.'

'I see.'

'Rannveig was holding a golf club in her right hand,' he continues.

'Rannveig?'

'Yes. She was putting a ball as she walked.'

I stare at Markús.

'You're positive?'

'Yes.'

'Did you speak to them?'

'Yes.'

'And what was their explanation for being out and about during the night?'

'Rannveig said she'd woken up and saw I wasn't in bed. So she got dressed and went out into the corridor to look for me. That's where she ran into her grandfather and they went for a short walk together – and she picked up a golf club to take with her.'

'Then what?'

'Rannveig and I said goodnight to Rögnvaldur and went

back inside and back to bed.'

'Did you go out again? Later that night?'

'No.'

'And Rannveig?'

'No. She didn't either.'

'You're sure?'

'Yes. She fell asleep right away.'

'And you?'

'I lay awake at her side until it was almost morning.'

I think for a while over Markús's new version of events.

'And how is this supposed to help you?'

'The two of them were walking away from the church at around the time the murders took place,' he replies. 'Surely that changes everything.'

'Are you really telling me that Rannveig and her grandfather committed the murders between them?'

'I'm just saying that I saw them outside with the golf club.'

'Which golf club?'

'The murder weapon.'

'Can you be certain she had that particular club?'

'I know my own clubs. She had the seven iron.'

I lean back in my chair.

'You're not thinking logically,' I say.

'I'm telling you what I saw.'

'Let's go back over this. You were in the yard at Skálholt at a quarter to two that night. That's around half an hour before the murders were committed.'

Markús nods.

'You saw Rannveig walking back to the building at that time with the murder weapon in her hand.'

'Yes.'

'Then she went straight to bed?'

'Yes.'

'And you were awake at her side for at least the next hour?'

'Yes.'

'So it's out of the question that she could be guilty of the murders.'

'Why?'

'Firstly, because the murders were committed after two o'clock. Secondly, the murder weapon was found in the grass not far from the church and the perpetrator had taken care to wipe all fingerprints off it.'

Markús sighs deeply.

'So what you're telling me is that the murderer took the golf club after Rannveig put it back in its place,' I continue. 'The police are going to continue to believe that you did it.'

He shakes his head.

''This will weaken your case, in my opinion,' I say.

'In what way?'

'You're confirming that you were outside in the yard very shortly before the murders were committed. And that the murder weapon was in your golf bag.'

Markús appears to have given up.

'I'm sorry. I didn't think this through.'

'All you're doing is providing Rannveig with a watertight alibi,' I say after a long silence.

'I am?'

'Do you have any reason to do so?'

'No. Not at all.'

'As far as I'm aware she hasn't been a suspect at any point.'

'Of course not. She loved her father with all her heart.'

'And she knew nothing of your affair with Jónína?'

'No.'

'Then she doesn't need an alibi, does she?'

'I've stopped being able to think straight in here,' he responds angrily. 'You're going to have to get me out before I go crazy.'

I have the feeling he's being overdramatic.

Or is it his time in solitary confinement that's left Markús so bewildered?

40

Outside the Litla Hraun prison I sit for a while in my silver steed. I'm no closer to understanding what Markús intends to achieve by changing his story.

There are two possibilities.

He's heading for a nervous breakdown, as he himself seems to think. Or else he suspects that Rannveig might have committed the murders at Thorláksbúð. He's doing everything he can to prevent that from being discovered. Is that supposed to be atonement for his own failings and betrayal?

I've no idea which it is. Time for the long route home. That includes calling at Thingvellir and grilling Rögnvaldur Rögnvaldsson.

He's sitting at a table in the garden, the same as last time I called on him.

The trees shade us from the sunshine.

I ask him straight out about his movements the night the murders took place.

The old guy confirms Markús's account. But there's one important extra element.

'Rannveig was considerably upset,' he says. 'She had woken shortly after one o'clock, wondered where her husband was and went to look for him. But she found me instead. I asked her to walk with me as it was a beautiful summer night and she agreed.'

'She took a golf club with her?'

'Yes. It was such a bright night it seemed ideal for a few putts, considering she was up anyway.'

'Do you always go to sleep so late?'

Rögnvaldur smiles.

'That's down to age,' he replies. 'For the last few years I've not slept more than two or three hours at night.'

'Did you see Markús?'

'Yes. He was smoking in the yard as we came back. Rannveig dislikes smoking, and she ticked him off before going inside to bed.'

'And Markús?'

'We walked together down to the car park, where we parted.'

'So he didn't go in with Rannveig?'

'No.'

'That's not what Markús says.'

Rögnvaldur makes no reply. He just watches me calmly.

'Am I right in thinking that you didn't stay at Skálholt?'

'That is correct. I drove home that night.'

'Why? Had you seen enough of the seminar?'

'I went primarily to listen to the presentations given by Rannveig and Markús. Both were on the first day of the seminar.'

'How did you hear of Thorsteinn's death?'

'I was here at home when Arnlaugur called me.'

Rögnvaldur's right hand goes to his chest and grimaces. It's as if he's in real pain.

'What's the matter?' I ask.

'I get an occasional feeling of discomfort in my chest, but it passes.'

I hold back with more questions for a moment. But I'm right back to it when the old guy appears to recover.

'How long did you and Markús talk out there that night?'

'At most ten minutes.'

'What did you talk about?'

Rögnvaldur pauses for thought.

'I recall that we discussed the bright summer weather and the harmful effects of smoking.'

'Anything else?'

'Yes, unfortunately.'

'Go on.'

'Markús asked if I had seen Jónína Katrín, and I told him truthfully that I had seen her go for a walk with Thorsteinn at around midnight.'

I stare at him in surprise.

'So Markús knew that she and Thorsteinn were together that night?'

'Yes.'

'Because you told him?'

'Yes.'

Rögnvaldur leans forward.

'At that point I unfortunately had no knowledge of the affair between Markús and Jónína Katrín,' he adds. 'These days I'm the last to find out things that people would prefer to keep quiet. Otherwise I would certainly have taken action long before.'

'Do you believe your words triggered Markús? Made him jealous?'

'That is undeniably my fear.'

'That he could have murdered your son and Jónína because of what you told him?'

'It's possible.'

Rögnvaldur's hand again goes to his chest.

He grimaces in pain. His right hand goes to his jacket pocket for a pill bottle. He drops it into the grass.

I'm on my feet, reach for the pills. I open it and put one in the old man's mouth.

Rögnvaldur swallows.

'Another,' he whispers. 'I need two.'

He reaches for a clear plastic bottle on the table and takes a drink of water.

I watch him for a while.

'That's the worst of it over,' he says at last. 'But just for the moment.'

'Don't you need to be in hospital?'

'Yes. I think you should call the emergency number.'

It's an hour later when an ambulance comes to a halt in the yard to take the old guy to the National Hospital on Hringbraut.

Lying on the stretcher, Rögnvaldur hands me his keys.

'I must rely on you to lock up the house,' he says. 'You should also let Rannveig know that I'll be at the National Hospital.'

When the ambulance is on its way to Reykjavík, I go indoors and make myself coffee in the kitchen. Then I call Rannveig.

Afterwards I take a seat in the garden, sipping black coffee. I'm making no progress in reaching a conclusion on guilt and innocence.

What Rögnvaldur has told me is another indicator that my client could be guilty of the Skálholt murders. On the other hand, Markús's new version of his testimony indicates the opposite – that he suspects his wife, or even Rögnvaldur.

Is everyone trying to deceive me?'

Máki's remark that Rögnvaldur had, and still has, a God-given talent for mendacity comes to mind.

Could his account of the conversation with Markús be complete fiction?

The anger's building inside me.

Is Rögnvaldur trying to fool me? Or is Markús?

Or both of them?

I take the coffee cup into the house. I wash it in the kitchen sink and place it on the draining board. Then I check that the windows are all securely locked, before going back to the front door.

Then I pull up short. I glance at the library door.

I'm alone here. I can do what I like.

I think it over before making a decision. I hurry to the library and find the remote control. The corner cabinet swings open. I clatter down the stairs where I watched Rögnvaldur open the combination lock a few days ago.

I close my eyes. All my mental energy goes into recalling the movements of Rögnvaldur's fingers. I open my eyes. Press the buttons in sequence. I hear the click as the door opens.

Bingo!

41

It's a very strange feeling being here in this secret archive. I feel as if I'm at the centre of an edifice of lies without much hope of stumbling across the door to truth.

I pass in front of the grey cabinets in Rögnvaldur Rögnvaldsson's insanely expensive underground bunker in the hope of catching sight of his son's briefcase. I'm confident that the old guy has been lying to me.

But the briefcase is nowhere to be seen.

I have no special interest in this collection of old documents relating to the political machinations of a bygone age. I'm no historian.

Unless?

I glance along the long row of cabinets, all marked with letters.

Where's G?

There are three of them.

Gunnsteinn Ástráðsson's file should be in the third of these.

I pull out one drawer after another until I find the right one.

It's slim and sparse. Just four typed sheets. Some have handwritten comments.

The oldest dates back to 1968 and is information about Gunnsteinn. By then he had already made the move from Raufarhöfn to Reykjavík some time before. It states that his parents are openly communists. Gunnsteinn is described as an artistic type who has published one book of poetry, that he's a member of the Movement. *'Unreliable sexual deviant,'* has been added in red in the margin. Under that, *Ófeigur Gunnarsson.*

Does this mean that Gunnsteinn and Ófeigur were a couple?

Surely that's a question that Örnólfur can answer, or maybe Hallbera.

The file contains a memo on two sheets of paper detailing Gunnsteinn's participation in the Movement's demonstrations. One of these was an occupation of the US military TV station up on Miðnesheiði that stopped transmission for a while. That was in 1969.

The last document is a request from the US embassy for assistance in locating a young man who stole important papers from a US official who was staying at Hótel Loftleiðir. The official isn't named. Underneath is a note to state that this refers to Gunnsteinn Ástráðsson, initialled by ThR and SA.

'Relevant information been delivered into the right hands,' it says in red ink. *'SA brought them together. Case concluded.'*

It's dated May and June 1973.

ThR?

Undoubtedly Thorsteinn Rögnvaldsson.

And SA?

Símon Andrésson? Was he also one of Rögnvaldur's errand boys?

There's another question that comes to mind.

Could this US official have been John Adam Cussler?

And what does *the right hands* mean?

I suspect that means the US embassy. Or the military police at the US base in Keflavík.

I take pictures of the documents with my phone. Then the folder goes back where it belongs.

So what about this Cussler? Isn't it likely that Rögnvaldur would have been aware of a visit from a high-ranking US secret service official at the height of the Cold War?

There are only three folders in the archive under C. One of these holds the information I'm looking for.

The oldest memo is from 1962. This relates that Rögnvaldur met scientist John Adam Cussler at the US embassy. During this conversation he expressed a strong interest in the research carried out by the late Björn Sigurðsson, the head of the University of Iceland's pathology research department at Keldur.

'Cussler requested my assistance in obtaining a sample of a virus that Björn had isolated and described in an English scientific journal some years ago.'

Further down, the word *'Concluded,'* appears in red ink.

The most recent document in the Cussler file is dated May 1973.

'Met Cussler at the embassy. Items stolen from him at Hótel Loftleiðir. Clear description of the culprit.'

Underneath this has been added, again in the same red ink, *'10th June. Culprit found. Case concluded.'*

I photograph these documents and think things over.

It appears to me that these papers indicate clearly that Gunnsteinn encountered Cussler at Hótel Loftleiðir and stole the ring from him on his way out. But he might have stolen other items that could have been even more important.

It's also clear that Rögnvaldur indicated to Cussler that

Gunnsteinn was the perpetrator – having been identified by Thorsteinn and Símon.

If so, how did the young man end up on the glacier?

I replace the folder in its cabinet, lock the basement and go back into the sunshine.

Rannveig calls in the afternoon.

'My grandfather isn't doing well.'

'Are you at the hospital?'

'Yes. But I need to go home later.'

'What do the doctors say?'

'That he doesn't have long to live.'

'Are they talking days or weeks?'

'Weeks, I hope. He's awake and alert.'

'Isn't that a good sign?'

'Yes, as far as that goes.'

'Let me know if there's anything you need.'

'OK.'

Then I call Máki. I tell him about Rögnvaldur's heart condition.

'Is he on his last legs?'

'According to the doctors. Unless he confounds all expectations and makes it to a hundred.'

'You reckon Rögnvaldur has some dirt on Death, like he does with everyone else?' Máki asks with a cold laugh.

I get busy at the office until almost five. Then it's time to fetch my daughter from nursery.

Lísa Björk stops me in the hall.

'I finally got an answer from the Ministry of Education in Belgrade,' she says with a worried look on her face.

'About time.'

'There's something strange going on.'

'How so?'

'They found a schoolteacher called Angjelo Skender Gjergji in their records,' Lísa Björk replies. 'The problem is that he's dead.'

'Dead?' I demand. 'When?'

'According to their records, he died in Kosovo in 1998.'

'That's at least a year before Alexander came to Iceland?'

'Yes. They say that this Gjergji was killed in a battle between Serbs and Albanians.'

'This has to be a misunderstanding.'

'I was naturally very surprised at this reply from them and

sent another message to ask if there might have been another teacher with this same name, but they say absolutely not. It's documented, they say, that Angjelo Skender Gjergji died in 1998.'

I stare at Lísa Björk.

'Then who the hell is Alexander?'

42

Tuesday 20th July 2010

Hospitals never agree with me.

The overwhelming smell is a dreadful reminder of how precarious life can be. It feels like the stench of death is coming at me from every direction.

Rögnvaldur is in a room of his own.

There's an oxygen mask on his face, drips in his left arm.

Rannveig is sitting on a chair at his side when I visit just before midday. I take both her hands in mine.

'How's your grandfather?'

'He's conscious, but he sleeps a lot of the time,' she replies.

'What do the doctors say?'

'Sometimes I don't think they know any more than we do.'

'But what do they say?'

'The one this morning said that if his condition remains stable, he could hold out for a few weeks or even months,' Rannveig replies. 'But he said he could also lapse into a coma at any moment.'

'So he could be unconscious for his final few weeks?'

'Exactly.'

'That was Rögnvaldur's fear. Living without knowing about it.'

'Yes. He told me that.'

The old guy opens his eyes.

He pulls the oxygen mask from his face when he sees us.

'Did I doze off?' he asks, his voice a whisper.

'You slept for a little while,' Rannveig tells him.

'Give me something to drink.'

He drinks through an orange straw, with difficulty.

Then he looks at me.

'You locked up securely?'

'Yes,' I say. 'Here are your keys.'

He gestures to the little bedside table.

'Open the drawer,' he whispers.

I do as he asks. There's a small black bag in the drawer.

'Put the keys in my bag,' he says.

I see that in the bag are various personal documents, and two more bunches of keys. There's also the will he showed me a copy of up at Thingvellir.

'This is the moment of truth.'

'That's not for sure, is it?'

'Yes. Rannveig will give you this bag when I've left this world, in mind or in body. Everything is to be as we agreed.'

'Of course.'

He looks at Rannveig.

'You ought to get something to eat,' he says.

'I'm not hungry.'

'Well, you need to take a break, my dear. Stella will stay here with me.'

'All right. I won't be long.'

'You must do everything in your power to protect Rannveig over the coming weeks and months,' Rögnvaldur continues when she has gone out into the corridor. 'Will you promise me that?'

'Yes, of course.'

'You'll have to protect her from everything.'

'What is there to fear?'

'I'm aware that the ghosts of the past lie everywhere in wait,' the old man replies. 'But you'll also have to protect her from her husband.'

'In what way?'

'She will have to divorce Markús Hálfdánarson, whether he's found guilty or not.'

'You mustn't forget that I also have an obligation to do my very best on my client's behalf to get him out of prison.'

Rögnvaldur is gasping.

He places the oxygen mask again over his face. He draws breath with difficulty, until his breathing steadies.

'I know you'll do what you have to,' he says. 'But it must never be at Rannveig's expense. You hear me?'

'You need have no fears in that respect,' I reply. 'I'll do everything I can to look after her interests.'

'Trusting you is a huge risk for me to take,' the old man says after a long silence. 'I do this only at the insistence of my granddaughter, my sole heir.'

'I won't let her down.'

'Everything you need to deal with my affairs in my absence is in that bag.'

Rögnvaldur again places the oxygen mask over his face.

I get to my feet.

I pace the floor slowly while he fights for breath. I'm doing my best to ignore the horrors hospitals give me.

'There's one last thing I want to say to you,' he whispers at last.

'What's that?'

'You might well get Markús acquitted due to the lack of evidence, but that's purely because nobody saw him carrying out his intentions at Thorláksbúð.'

'You believe he's guilty?'

Rögnvaldur again gasps for breath. His hands flail.

I grab the oxygen mask. Put it over his face. I call out for the nursing team to help, and they usher me out of the room.

43

Thursday 22nd July 2010

I'm on the way to the north coast.

My cousin Sissi's sitting beside me in the silver steed. His hair's cropped close and he's sporting a cool pair of shades.

Lísa Björk was totally opposed to me going alone and with no back-up to confront Alexander, the yard manager at Gullinhamrar.

'We know nothing about this man's past,' she said. 'He could have been a highly dangerous criminal in Kosovo.'

I have to admit that we have no idea who Alexander was back home in the Balkans. But I don't have many choices.

'I don't dare trust the cops with this information,' I said firmly. 'At best, they'll arrest Alexander and deport him to Serbia or Kosovo. Then we'll never know if he encountered Julia at Gullinhamrar in the summer of 2001.'

'We can't set it as a condition that he's first interviewed about that side of it?' Lísa Björk asked.

'It could be too late. Why would Alexander answer the cops' questions about Julia if he knows he's going to be deported back to Kosovo anyway?'

'Yes, that's open to doubt. Most likely he has nothing to gain by doing that.'

'I don't want to take that risk. We have a unique opportunity to force Alexander to tell us the truth. There won't be any second chance.'

Lísa Björk finally accepted my reasoning that I'd have to use this information myself to force the yard manager into a corner.

'But you'll have to take precautions,' she said.

I agreed to play it as safe as possible.

My cousin Sissi is my insurance. Plus he's a tech wizard *par excellence*.

'You'll need to ensure that your conversation is recorded securely,' he said yesterday when I explained what I had in mind.

'How do we do that?'

'You need to have a tiny cordless camera hidden about your person,' Sissi replied. 'It sees and hears everything that you see and hear, and it transmits the data to a computer that's in your car.'

'Can you fix this by tonight?'

Sissi nodded. And he agreed to go with me up north to ensure that nothing would go wrong with the recording.

The camera is hidden in a large star-shaped amulet hung from a necklace. It dangles over the pink Armani top that complements my snug leather trousers.

By the time we pass Sauðárkrókur and approach Gullinhamrar, clouds have obscured the bright sunshine.

I bring the silver steed to a halt on the gravel in front of the farmhouse, beside a huge black 4x4 and a newish quad bike. Below the stables are four horses behind the robust paddock fence.

There's no sign of Alexander, Geiri Sveins or his brother Jósteinn anywhere. There aren't even any of the youngsters who spend summers working at the stable.

Sissi waits in the car while I knock at the door.

No answer.

More than likely Geiri is up in the Highlands, taking a riding tour up to Askja. It's that time of year.

But where's the stables guy?

'I'm going to walk up to the stable,' I tell Sissi.

'Hold on,' he says, waking up the laptop that's in his hands.

I glance up at the Gullinhamrar pasture where hay bales lie in their green wrapping here and there after the first harvest of the summer. I look over the new stable and the barn, the old concrete-walled house that now looks barely habitable, the silage tower and the ruins of the old outhouses beneath the sheer cliffs that give the farm its name.

'Say something,' Sissi calls out.

'Double Jack D!'

'OK,' he replies. 'Picture and sound are clear.'

I lock the car and walk towards the stable block. I'm almost there when Alexander appears in the doorway.

He marches quickly towards me.

'Looking for a horse?' he asks.

'No.'

It's clearly at that very moment that he recognises me. He stops abruptly.

'What do you want now?'

'I want the truth,' I reply.

He pulls a phone from the pocket of his dark blue boiler suit.

'I'm calling Jósteinn,' he says.

'Listen to me first,' I say. 'It's worth your while.'

Alexander hesitates, the phone in his hand.

'Worth it, how?' he asks.

'I know who you aren't,' I respond.

'I don't get you.'

'I know that you aren't Angjelo Skender Gjergji. He was killed in Kosovo in 1998.'

The yard manager's face turns pale. There's hostility in his dark eyes that stare at me.

'The authorities in Serbia have confirmed Gjergji's death in an email to me,' I add. 'If I forward that email to the Directorate of Immigration, they'll kick you out of the country. You'll be handed over to the authorities in Kosovo or Serbia.'

Alexander stands completely still. His face is rigid. That could be either fear or anger.

'I suggest we do a deal,' I continue.

'What sort of deal?'

'I'm prepared to forget the email I received from Belgrade if you tell me what happened when Julia arrived here on her motorcycle nine years ago.'

He looks at me for a long time before saying anything.

'I don't know what happened,' he says at last.

'I don't believe that.'

'It's the truth.'

'Then I'll have no choice but to forward that message to the Directorate of Immigration.'

'No. No, don't do that.'

I take my phone from my pocket.

'The offer still stands,' I retort coldly, brandishing the phone. 'But not for long.'

Alexander wets his lips with the tip of his tongue.

'I don't know what happened. That's the truth,' he says earnestly. 'But I can show you her motorbike.'

'Julia's motorcycle?'

'Yes.'

Eureka!

44

I watch Alexander in excitement as he fidgets in front of me in his black rubber boots and blue overalls.

There's no hiding that he's a bundle of nerves.

'Where's this motorcycle?' I ask, breaking the silence.

'Up there.'

He gestures towards the cliffs at the top of the pasture.

'In those ruins?'

'The bike's hidden in a cave behind the old building,' he replies. 'That's the truth.'

'Show me. You go ahead.'

He hesitates for a moment. Then he turns his back on me as he strides up the pasture.

I follow, keeping a reasonable distance.

We pass a few of the green hay bales on the way up to the ancient outhouses that look to have been built against the cliff face.

The gable has at one time been fastened to the rocks with heavy wire that has long since turned dark brown with years of rust. Part of the roof has half fallen in, and the bent and corroded sheets of corrugated iron are visible as we approach.

This seems to be nothing more than a ruin rather than a usable building. All the same, there's a heavy lock on the door.

Alexander feels for the heavy bunch of keys at his belt, opens the door and pulls at the handle.

'It's in there,' he says.

'You go first,' I reply.

He hesitates. Then he shrugs and steps over the dirty threshold.

I stop in the doorway. In the gloom, I glance around. I see old feed troughs that extend all the way up to the rock.

Some of them are in pieces.

This place was clearly used as a byre in the old days. That was back when there were still sheep at Gullinhamrar.

'Where's the bike?' I ask once more.

Alexander goes up to the cliff face. He stops next to a large door made of coarse timber. This one also has a heavy padlock.

'Inside here,' he says.

'Open the door.'

He obeys.

Behind the door is a large opening in the rocky cliff face.

'Is there a light in there?'

The stables manager steps inside the cave and comes back with a torch in his hand.

I follow him into the cave that feels surprisingly roomy. At this end the ceiling is high and there's plenty of space between the walls. But the further we go, the lower the headroom quickly becomes.

Farmers at Gullinhamrar appear to have used the cave as a storeroom for years or even decades, as the place is full of all kinds of junk. There are huge tyres, old tools and all sorts of electrical stuff.

'Show me the motorcycle,' I repeat.

Alexander goes over to the left where the cave becomes even narrow and tighter. He finally stops and trains the beam of the torch on a pile of ropes and riding tack stacked against the wall.

'I don't see a motorcycle.'

'It's under there,' he replies.

'Take that stuff off.'

He hesitates again.

'Put the torch on the floor.'

The stables manager puts the torch down. He looks at me as if he's checking out his options. Then he turns back to the junk in the corner of the cave.

Crouching down, I snatch the torch up. I take a few steps back to be sure. The light shines on the pile.

Alexander shifts the ropes and tack further up the cave.

Finally I see the outline of black tyres.

Wow!

Maybe this guy's telling me the truth.

Restless and impatient, I wait while he moves the rest of the junk away from the bike.

'Lift it up!'

He takes hold of the handlebars and the seat, then stands it up.

I search for the manufacturer's name on the side. It jumps out at me almost right away.

Kawasaki.

This could certainly be her bike.

'All right,' I say. 'Is there any more of Julia's stuff here?'

'There could be,' he says.

I come closer to shine the light into the corner of the cave.

Alexander takes his chance and shoves the bike with great strength straight into me.

I'm taken unawares. I drop the torch. I'm thrown backwards and land hard on the coarse floor of the cave.

Shit!

The stables manager from Kosovo takes to his heels.

He pushes past me as I lie flat on the jagged floor. He rushes out of the cave and slams the door behind him.

I hear the click of the padlock as he locks me in.

Fucking hell!

45

I sit up and shake my head.

Then I get my phone from my trouser pocket. I call my cousin Sissi who's hopefully been watching what's happening in the cave.

'Is the recording clear?' I demand.

'Yes. It's fine.'

'The bastard locked me in. Can you see him?'

'He's running over to the old farmhouse,' Sissi reports.

'He mustn't get away.'

'What do you want me to do?'

'Just do your best to hold him up,' I reply.

I end the call and then call Ragnar Jónatansson's number.

'Call me later,' the chief superintendent says. 'I'm in a meeting.'

'This is life or death,' I gasp.

'What's up?'

'I found Julia MacKenzie's motorcycle,' I blurt out. 'They've no doubt hidden her body somewhere here as well.'

'Where are you?'

'At Gullinhamrar.'

Fat Raggi doesn't believe me. I have to explain twice.

'Alexander caught me off guard and I'm locked in this fucking cave where they hid the motorcycle,' I add angrily. 'He's making his escape while you're keeping me talking.'

'Take it easy,' he says. 'We're on the case.'

I stow the phone back in my pocket and reach for the torch. I get to my feet and rush over to the door. I kick the wooden door hard with the soles of my shoes.

The door doesn't move.

Tools!

I need something big and heavy to batter it with.

Shining the light around, I check out the junk that's strewn like driftwood all around the cave.

Aha!

I catch sight of an old, rusty sledgehammer.

The shaft has broken off. But there's enough left of it to be usable.

I put the torch down on the floor. I raise the sledgehammer and let one blow after another rain down on the rough timber.

Again and again and again.

The effort leaves me drenched in sweat. The power of sheer anger keeps me going.

Finally, at long last, enough of the planks are broken to let me squeeze out through the gap and into the old outhouse.

I call Sissi again.

'Where's Alexander?'

'He's starting the jeep.'

'Head him off!'

'You took the car keys,' he says calmly.

'Hell!'

I sprint through the ruins of the building.

Alexander is reversing the jeep out of the yard in front of the new farmhouse when I come running down the pasture.

I run for the silver steed.

Sissi sees me coming and opens the driver's door.

The black jeep's about to turn onto the road as I haul my car around in a half-circle in the gravel and put my foot down hard. The tyres howl on the dirt road's surface, kicking up dust that surrounds us like a storm cloud.

He's heading north.

'Where's the bastard going?'

'He's not making for Sauðárkrókur, that's for sure.'

I hand Sissi my phone.

'Call Lísa Björk,' I tell him. 'Make sure she's in touch with Raggi.'

I'm on the black jeep's tail.

Alexander isn't hanging around. But the silver steed is steadily closing the gap. It's raring to go like a racehorse that doesn't know the meaning of coming second.

He's driving fast on the coast road leading north.

'Where does this road go?'

'First out to Skagatá, from there to Skagaströnd and Blönduós and then onto Highway One,' Sissi replies.

There's no more than a few metres between the cars.

Alexander must realise that he's not getting away from me. I'll always be on his tail. Like a vengeful witch.

What will his desperation make him do?

He could easily do something crazy, like braking hard in the hope of wrecking my silver steed.

It's a risk I have to take.

He could also make a serious mistake. He could lose control of the jeep.

We hurtle along the coast road at an insane speed in this mad race. I keep the silver steed as close as I dare.

It's just as well there's no other traffic. But I know that could change at any moment.

'There's a truck coming the other way!' Sissi yells.

Alexander has clearly noticed it too late.

He swerves to avoid a collision. But he's in the loose gravel at the side of the road. Like an idiot, he stamps hard on the brakes.

The black jeep is hurled off the road. It rolls over and over on its way towards the sea. It ends up on the rocky shore.

I stop the silver steed by the side of the road. I jump out and hurry down to the shore where the jeep lies on its side.

Alexander is held in by the seatbelt.

There's blood on his face. But he's conscious.

I go to the front of the jeep. I stare at him through the shattered windscreen.

'Tell me where you buried Julia's body,' I say.

Alexander looks back at me with a wild glint in his eye.

Then he starts to laugh like a maniac.

'You'll never find a body at Gullinhamrar,' he says, alternately coughing and laughing. 'Never. Not ever.'

46

A hell of a day!

I allow myself to sink deep into the snow-white bathtub in my room at the hotel in Sauðárkrókur, with a glass of Jack D on the chair. I take the first sip of the day and groan with delight.

It's just before midnight and the events of the day have left me battered and bruised.

Alexander is in hospital. The doctors say that with the injuries sustained in the crash it could go either way. But they've spent a lot of time trying to stitch him back together.

The cops tried to question him in the ambulance, but he'd drifted out of consciousness before they could get anything useful out of him.

On the other hand, they've been poring over my recording of the conversation with Gullinhamrar's yard manager. They have his admission that he knew about Julia MacKenzie's motorcycle and proof that he showed me the evidence there in the cave.

The motorcycle is irrefutable evidence that the British geology student called at Gullinhamrar in the summer of 2001. It's just as Birkir Brynjólfsson assured me a month ago. And exactly as I informed the boys in black.

The presence of the motorcycle also indicates that she didn't get away from this alive.

So where's the body?

I told the cops of the yard manager's scornful assertion that no body would ever be found at Gullinhamrar. That was part of my detailed report on the events of the day.

A forensics team from the police in Reykjavík started examining the place that afternoon. They'll still be working there tomorrow.

By evening, they were able to confirm that Julia MacKenzie had travelled to Iceland on the motorcycle that had been hidden in the cave.

But the city's finest have sadly not been able to identify any of her other belongings, let alone anything that could lead to where the body might be buried.

I have a long phone call with Fat Raggi this evening.

The chief superintendent hauls me over the coals for failing to pass on to him the information from the ministry in Serbia that the Kosovan yard manager at Gullinhamrar had come to Iceland under a dead man's identity. But he's effusive in his praise for my dogged determination to search for Julia.

'You can do things that we can't,' he says, as if that's an excuse for his colleagues' inertia.

Then I call Julia's uncle. I tell him what I've found.

He's both pleased and saddened.

He's glad because it looks like his sister will finally get to know what happened to her only daughter, after nine years of waiting.

But he's devastated, as finding her motorcycle seems to finally confirm the family's fear that Julia's trip to Iceland cost her her life.

'My sister has always lived in the hope that Julia could be alive somewhere, that she could've lost her memory or some such circumstances,' Gregory George MacKenzie says. 'I've often told her that it's not realistic to expect that sort of possibility, but she clung on tight to her hope. Although I welcome, of course, what you have achieved, it saddens me deeply that I have to give her such sad news.'

The city's finest have grilled Gullinhamrar's owner Jósteinn Sveinsson well into the evening. They say they'll continue tomorrow.

They're not saying a word. But Raggi let fall that Jósteinn has denied any involvement in Julia's disappearance. He's adamant that he knew nothing about the motorcycle hidden at his farm.

'But Birkir Brynjólfsson was certain that Jósteinn was there when Julia called,' I say. 'That's laid out in his signed testimony that I handed over to you weeks ago.'

'All I can tell you, and in strict confidence, is that Jósteinn seems determined to blame Alexander for everything,' the chief superintendent said.

'Then it's even more important that the yard manager stays alive.'

'The doctors aren't optimistic.'

'I feel it's going to be a shit outcome if Jósteinn Sveinsson gets away scot-free due to lack of evidence.'

'They consider it likely that Alexander could regain consciousness, even if only briefly,' Raggi said. 'We just have to wait and hope.'

I also fielded a call from Máki earlier in the evening.

'Congratulations,' he said. 'I just need a comment from you

to finish off a news item about how the cops messed up the Julia MacKenzie investigation.'

'Can't it wait until tomorrow?'

'Preferably not.'

I gave him a few words he could quote. Then I made for the snow-white bathtub.

The hot water gradually draws out the tension left by the day's exertion. And Jack D warms me like never before.

I finally manage to relax after a day of tumult and nervous energy.

My cousin Sissi is already asleep. As is Sóley Árdís, being looked after by Cora back home in the south.

So it's just me with my own company, as so often.

My thoughts drift gradually from the shattering events of the day.

I move on to pleasant memories. Of sweet encounters.

Touch and imagination are all that's needed, as Mother said.

47

Friday 23rd July 2010

There's an unexpected guest at the hotel's breakfast table.

It's Alfreð Sveinsson, the half-brother of Geiri and Jósteinn from Gullinhamrar, who was formerly Sauðárkrókur's chief superintendent of police at the time of Julia MacKenzie's disappearance.

He's clearly deeply distressed.

'I could hardly believe my ears when I heard the news yesterday evening,' he says.

'The truth can sometimes be hard to accept,' I reply.

'I feel I ought to tell you that I'd no idea the British girl had gone to Gullinhamrar,' he continues. 'At the time we were searching I had none of the information that's now come to light.'

'Really?'

'Yes, really. Unfortunately. All the same, I feel I've let her and her family down. I can't tell you how sorry I am.'

'How could your half-brothers have kept this quiet all that time?'

'In my opinion it's very unlikely that Geiri had anything to do with this,' Alfreð says.

'But he's been living at Gullinhamrar all these years.'

'The Albanian must be the one who bears responsibility for all this.'

'And Jósteinn?'

'Jósteinn has struggled for years with a serious booze problem, and he can get furiously angry when the drink gets the better of him. But he's never been charged with assault or any other violent crime.'

'That doesn't mean a thing.'

'Please don't interpret my words as any kind of expiation for my half-brothers. If they knew of the motorcycle in the cave at Gullinhamrar, then at best they're guilty as accessories to a crime and deserve whatever punishment comes their way.'

When the old guy has assuaged his conscience, Sissi and I go up to the police station where the forensic team have set up their base.

They're making an early start. They're already at work up at Gullinhamrar.

We head out there.

There's a gloom over Skagafjörður and the surrounding district. Drizzle fills the air at Gullinhamrar. It's as if nature is expressing its sympathy.

The forensic team has finished its work in the cave and the old concrete-walled building.

'We're moving on to the farmhouse and the stables, and hope to be finished tonight,' says the inspector in charge, an amiable, dark-haired guy of around thirty.

He won't divulge whether or not any of Julia's belongings have come to light. So I call Fat Raggi. He confirms that nothing has been found so far.

I remind him of the photo taken up at Askja by the couple from Blönduós, which showed clearly that Julia had a backpack, and two bags fitted to the motorcycle.

'None of those bags have been found so far,' he replies.

'That seems odd.'

'Alexander could have buried them.'

'Or he and Jósteinn between them.'

'Jósteinn denies any knowledge at all of Julia's presence at Gullinhamrar.'

'He's lying. That's a cast-iron certainty.'

My cousin Sissi and I walk up the pasture. But we get no further than the tumbledown shed built over the entrance to the cave.

The doors are cordoned off with yellow police incident tape.

We go back the way we came and head towards the old house and the silage tower.

I notice two ventilation pipes emerging from the ground not far from the house. They're a clear indicator of an underground septic tank.

A fair-haired youngster is saddling a young horse in the paddock in front of the stable.

'Are you going out riding?' he asks.

I chat with him for a while about working at Gullinhamrar – and his experience of dealing with Alexander and Jósteinn.

'Alexander is fine. But Jósteinn's drunk a lot of the time,' he replies.

'Does anyone live in the old house?'

'Yes. That's where Alexander sleeps.'

'Is that silage tower used?'

'They've sometimes talked about converting it into a guesthouse.'

'But there are no windows.'

'Some tourists get a kick out of staying in weird places.'

'I don't see a door anyway.'

'Access is through the old house.'

'Really? A tunnel, or something?'

'Well, something like that. I've never looked.'

'But nothing has come of the conversion idea, or what?'

'Not since I first came here last summer. But they've occasionally tinkered with outfitting the tower. '

'They? Who's they?'

'Alexander and Jósteinn.'

I get a dark suspicious feeling. It's instinctive and sudden.

'Come on,' I say to Sissi.

He follows me up to the house. We're stopped again by the bright yellow tape that tells us to keep out.

'Right. Stay here,' I tell him.

The door isn't locked.

Alexander has been living on the ground floor. There's a couple of small rooms – a kitchen, living room, bedroom and a bathroom with a shower cubicle.

A heavy door that appears to lead to a basement is locked.

I hesitate in front of the door, and then I call Raggi.

He listens to what I have to tell him.

'Hold on while I speak to the inspector at the scene,' he says.

The chief superintendent calls back four minutes later.

'Keli's on his way over to you,' he says.

'I'll wait for him here.'

The inspector's sulky after being called by the chief superintendent down south.

'We've already checked the basement,' he complains.

'And the tunnel to the silage tower?'

'What tunnel?'

I take that as a no.

He has Alexander's and Jósteinn's keys in his jacket pocket. I follow him down the steps to the cellar.

'Where's this tunnel supposed to be?' Keli asks.

'It's here somewhere.'

There are no windows down here.

There's a laundry room, and a freezer half-full of meat. And there's a store with some booze and cans of soft drinks.

I look around. I pay special attention to the side of the cellar that faces the silage tower. I see no doors.

A sideboard in the storeroom stands against the wall.

I examine it carefully.

Finally I come across a button behind a case of red wine. There's a click as I press it.

'There you go,' I say, and step aside.

Keli gazes into the dark tunnel in front of him. Then he calls his colleagues who arrive in ones and twos.

They talk among themselves.

'We'll check this out,' he says with a note of authority in his voice.

Then he disappears with another officer into the passage.

I hurry behind them with my heart in my mouth.

48

Keli switches on two bright lightbulbs that hang from the ceiling of the tunnel between the old house and the silage tower.

The walls of the tunnel have been panelled with plywood.

At the end is a heavy fire door.

Keli tries several of the keys before he finds the right one.

He steps over the threshold and feels for a light switch.

Two lights on the wall come to life.

The tower has been insulated inside all the way around and the walls clad in pine, painted in a pale shade. The ceiling height is a maximum of two metres. Two leather armchairs and a dark wood coffee table occupy the floor. There's also a TV stand with a newish flat screen television, a CD player and a handful of discs.

I look around the little tower living room. All I feel is deep disappointment. It seems out of the question that Julia MacKenzie's body could be hidden in this place.

Behind one of the armchairs is a spiral staircase that leads up to the next level. The hatch at the top of the steps is padlocked. It's a similar lock to the ones used to keep the doors leading to the cave shut up tight.

Keli's the first one up the stairs. He finds the right key for the padlock, raises the hatch and clambers up to the upper level.

I follow the inspector.

The upstairs section is also outfitted and panelled in pine painted the same pale colour. But the furniture is different.

There's a bed here. There's a bedside table, a wardrobe, a little cabinet opening at the top.

The bedclothes are untidy. It's as if someone slept here recently.

There are a few apples and oranges on the table.

I go to the little cabinet and lift the lid.

It's a toilet.

'You shouldn't be here,' Keli says.

The wardrobe is closed. It's locked.

'Is there a key for this?' I ask, without responding to the inspector's comment.

He tries several keys on both Alexander's and Jósteinn's key rings before he finds the right one. Both doors swing open.

The wardrobe is full of clothes. Some garments hang on clothes hangers and others are stuffed onto a shelf above.

I'm startled.

'All women's clothes,' I say.

'True,' Keli agrees.

A heavy, grey duvet lies at the bottom of the wardrobe.

'You're going to have to leave the scene,' the inspector repeats. 'Your presence is totally against all our rules of procedure.'

Stooping down quickly, I snatch away the duvet.

An unconscious woman lies on the floor. She's bound and gagged.

It's the long, red-brown hair, even though it's unkempt, that tells me who this is.

This is Julia MacKenzie. No doubt about it.

The face is the same as in the picture that I examined so carefully on my computer screen when this investigation began.

But she's very pale. Her arms and legs are thin.

The inspector is speechless. He stares dumbstruck into the wardrobe.

I put a finger to Julia's neck. There's a faint pulse.

'She's alive,' I say.

'Thank God!'

'We need a doctor, an ambulance and a helicopter. Right this fucking moment!'

Keli makes calls.

I tease the tape from Julia's mouth. Then I free her hands and feet.

She mutters something, still unconscious.

'Help me move her,' I call out.

The inspector lifts her head and shoulders, and I take her legs. Between us we place her gently on the bed.

I pull the duvet over Julia, who's wearing only underclothes.

'Julia? Julia?' I call to her, until she opens her eyes.

'You're safe now,' I tell her in English. 'Free and safe.'

It seems to take her a long time to understand what's being said to her.

'Free and safe!'

The tears trickle down her cheeks.

'Free and safe,' I say repeatedly, stroking her head.

Julia is still in a daze when the doctor appears.

'She appears to have been heavily sedated or drugged,' I say.

177

The doctor gets to work on Julia right away.

I take the opportunity to call Raggi. He's already spoken to the inspector.

'The chopper's on its way north,' he says immediately. 'She'll be taken to A&E at the National Hospital.'

'That's good.'

'It's a hell of a miracle, finding her alive like that,' the chief superintendent adds.

An hour later I watch as the helicopter lifts off from the Gullinhamrar pasture and heads south.

I finally have time to call Gregory George MacKenzie to give him the good news.

'Julia alive?' he asks, stunned. 'Alive?'

'Yes. She's been held captive all these years. She's on the way to hospital in Reykjavík right now.'

'How am I supposed to believe this?'

'I recognised her immediately from the photos,' I say. 'It's Julia.'

'God bless you.'

Once MacKenzie has got over the shock of such unexpected news, he's already organising the next step.

'I'll put off everything else,' he says. 'I'll be on the way to Reykjavík tonight with my own doctor and care team.'

'That sounds good.'

'See you in Reykjavík!'

My cousin Sissi gazes at me with frank admiration in his eyes.

'You're one of a kind,' he says.

I smile demurely. I agree entirely with his sentiment.

49

Saturday 24th July 2010

Julia MacKenzie was on her way home at around seven this evening. That's just about nine years since her trip to Iceland began.

Her adventure turned into a horrific nightmare.

Gregory George MacKenzie has been as good as his word.

The private jet he dispatched landed at Reykjavík airport late last night. He was on board in person, along with a doctor and two nurses.

I met him at the intensive care department at the National Hospital shortly afterwards.

He clasped my hands tight in his. His head dipped low.

'Nothing I can say or do can ever suffice for such a wonderful gift,' he said, deeply moved. 'My sister was in tears when I gave her the news.'

He'd already been to see his niece. He wanted to whisk her away to Britain that night.

But the city's finest were having none of it.

'We need her to make a preliminary statement concerning everything that happened before she leaves the country,' Ragnar Jónatansson said.

The British businessman did his best to get the chief superintendent to change his mind. But he wouldn't budge.

'She has to bear witness against those who held her captive,' Raggi said firmly. 'That's the most certain way to ensure they stay on remand for a long period.'

I added my own contribution to the discussion.

'I'm sure Julia will want to see the kidnappers properly punished,' I said. 'It should be possible to have completed her statement by around midday tomorrow, surely?'

'I expect so,' the chief superintendent replied. 'But then she'll also have to testify at the trial when it comes to it.'

MacKenzie finally agreed to our suggestions.

I met him again at the hospital early this morning.

'Julia spoke to her mother on the phone last night,' he said, holding back a sob. 'This has been the best moment of my life.'

The interview lasted well into the day, not least because the boys in black had to take frequent breaks.

Time and again Julia's emotions overwhelmed her, especially as she described her awful life as a captive in the tower at Gullinhamrar.

The nightmare began shortly after Jósteinn Sveinsson offered to take her out riding from Gullinhamrar. That was the day she disappeared.

He dismounted after riding for an hour or so, by the side of a river to the north of the steepest cliffs. They sat on a grassy knoll by the river and chatted about what could be seen from there.

Jósteinn had been drinking, and he was still swigging from a flask.

He tried to persuade her to drink with him, but she refused repeatedly and he took that badly.

'But I didn't expect anything bad,' Julia said. 'Then he suddenly jumped on me. I fought back as hard as I could, but he was too big and strong for me.'

That was the first rape of many.

Afterwards he punched her. She lost consciousness and didn't come round until that night.

By then she was already a prisoner in the tower.

Jósteinn Sveinsson and Alexander abused Julia all through those years. Sometimes together.

She was their plaything and sex slave.

Every attempt Julia made to escape was hopeless. There was one occasion when she almost managed to free herself from captivity at Gullinhamrar.

She took the opportunity when Jósteinn passed out drunk in the bed on the upper floor of the tower.

But Alexander noticed her make her way through the old farmhouse after emerging from the tunnel.

He showed her no mercy. He punished her with a beating and sent her back.

The rescue of Julia MacKenzie attracted instant media attention around the world.

Journalists and cameras, both newspaper and online media, were outside the National Hospital early that morning. More and more from other countries arrived as the day wore on.

MacKenzie was determined to shield Julia from the media attention.

'But I'll have to give them a short statement and I'd like you to be at my side,' he said.

I agreed to his request.

180

It was certainly a strange feeling to be facing such a horde of excited hacks – all those intrusive lenses, all those inquisitive faces.

MacKenzie read out a statement in English.

He described his niece's disappearance, and the fruitless search in the summer of 2001. He spoke of his sister's illness and her entreaty that he make one more attempt to find out what had become of her daughter.

'Her rescue is a miracle worked by a real person,' he said with a tear in his eye. 'The person who worked this miracle is standing beside me. Julia's freedom has been regained thanks to Stella Blómkvist.'

I had no choice but to say a few words in English when the babble of questions from the newsmen and the flashes of cameras hit me like an avalanche.

I tried to say a few measured words about the value of feminine insight and intuition. That would've put me on the right track. But I had to add something about the importance of not giving up, even when you're struggling to make progress.

'In this case it seemed that every avenue was blocked solid,' I said. 'But I never give up, for the simple reason that there's always some other route. Julia's being set free is evidence that it always pays to keep going, even when the outlook is bleak.'

I hug Julia before she's taken out to the ambulance.

She's weak, exhausted. But better things await her.

That evening Rannveig and I watch the foreign news bulletins showing the press conference in front of the National Hospital's doors. Then there are the sequences showing the ambulance that took Julia and her people to Reykjavík airport.

'Now you get to be world famous for fifteen minutes,' Rannveig says with a smile.

She's prepared a wonderful dinner for us. Sóley Árdís does her best to carry everything to the table. They've really clicked.

That bodes well.

I switch off all the phones upstairs. I'm determined to not let the rest of the world trouble me any more today.

The evening is ours. And the sweet delights of the night ahead await us.

50

Saturday 14th August 2010

A barefoot Sóley Árdís chases a multi-coloured ball through the dry grass of the garden.

'She's a delightful child,' my mother says, her voice thick with emotion.

I had no choice but to take time off when Richard Moreno called me from his office, a few days after I found Julia MacKenzie bound and gagged in the silage tower at Gullinhamrar.

He's my mother's second husband.

They met at the hotel my parents ran in the east of Iceland, Hótel Klettur. In my thoughts that place is shrouded in the dark shadows of the past.

We'd both had enough of the old man's domineering and violence.

When I left home to start studying at the Laugarvatn secondary college, she also said goodbye and moved to Florida.

She never returned to the place that had been home.

Neither did I. Except that once, to bury Karl Blómkvist.

Richard told me that my mother is seriously ill. He asked if I'd come with my daughter and stay for a while with them, to say our farewells.

We've been at their house in Orlando for a week. It's a beautiful detached house, all on one level. It has a large, lush garden. It's also close to the golf course where they've spent so much time walking in the sunshine.

Mum is in a bad way after a stroke. Most of her left side is paralysed. Her face is affected as well. But she can still get around the house and garden in her computerised wheelchair.

Richard looks after her well. It's just as well he's wealthy enough to afford the nurses who care for her morning and evening.

'Otherwise she'd have to be in a hospice, and I don't want that,' he said.

I've often been angry with my mother. Firstly, because she didn't give me the support I needed in taking on the old man out there in the east. Secondly, for running away to America and leaving me behind.

It's forgiven but not forgotten.

But she found what she was looking for in Florida.

Love and devotion.

Can I really criticise her for following her heart?

'I couldn't live any longer at Klettur,' she said by way of apology. 'And I knew that you'd be able to look after yourself.'

Of course she couldn't have known that.

But I keep quiet. It's not as if I'm going to see her again.

Lísa Björk is holding the fort at the legal practice while I'm out of the country. She sends me a daily email listing activity and events.

Not much takes me by surprise.

The media storm that broke with a bang following the discovery of Julia MacKenzie has faded away. There's nothing as stale in people's minds as yesterday's news. It always gives way to something fresh.

Gregory George MacKenzie has invited me to visit his family in Scotland, to meet Julia again, and her mother.

'Muriel wants to thank you in person,' he said when he called.

I promised to stop over in Glasgow on the way back to Iceland.

Máki called the day before yesterday.

'People can't believe that nobody suspected there was anything going on at Gullinhamrar, considering the number of people who go riding there every summer,' he said. 'I'm no longer the only one who's demanding that the Minister of Justice orders an official inquiry into the police's lousy handling of this investigation, even though I was the first to say so.'

Jósteinn Sveinsson and Alexander are both on remand.

'I can hardly believe that Geiri didn't know about the prisoner in the tower,' Máki continued. 'So I feel it's incomprehensible that the police didn't request to hold him on remand as well.'

'What's their explanation?'

'They state that Julia doesn't recall ever having seen him at Gullinhamrar.'

The city's finest still don't know who Alexander was back in Kosovo. But they've sent his fingerprints to the authorities in both Belgrade and Pristina. He refuses to give any information about his past. He's adamant that he's Angjelo Skender Gjergji.

Rannveig calls in the afternoon.

183

'I'm making good progress on editing the film,' she says. 'I heard from state TV and they expect to show the programme in November or December.'

'Great.'

Her grandfather's condition is unchanged. He fell into a coma after my last visit to the hospital and he's still unconscious.

'I'm flying to Scotland tomorrow, and home on Wednesday,' I tell her.

'Looking forward to seeing you,' she replies.

Richard orders a feast for our last evening in Florida.

My mother doesn't eat much, but can't take her eyes off my daughter, who eats heartily.

When the nurse has helped my mother to bed, Sóley Árdís and I sit for a long time at her bedside. She pats my daughter's head with her right hand, the side that still obeys her brain's instructions.

'I'm so pleased I got to see her before it's too late,' she says with tears in her eyes. 'And you, too.'

I nod.

'I have to tell you that I often doubted that I was doing the right thing,' she adds. 'So often I felt bad for having let you down.'

I wet my lips but say nothing.

'But after meeting Richard, there was nothing for it in my mind but to follow him to the ends of the earth. That's just the way it was. He saved me and brought me more happiness than I ever deserved.'

'Doesn't everyone deserve happiness?'

'Sometimes it's at the expense of someone else, and I'm truly sorry.'

I lean forward.

'Don't worry about us,' I reply. 'I'm an expert at looking out for myself, as you said. And Sóley Árdís couldn't be better looked after.'

'I can see she's so happy and clever.'

My mother tires quickly.

Sóley Árdís kisses her grandmother's cheek.

'Thank you for such a lovely time,' Mum says.

'Good night.'

We go to bed early, but I struggle to get to sleep.

Reminiscences of miserable teenage years keep me awake. These are the memories that still cause me pain and anger.

It goes without saying that the old man was the culprit.

Not my mother.

But I've never found it easy to forgive those who hurt me. I know that I'll never, ever forgive the old man, even though he's long dead.

But my mother at least had a decent excuse for making her escape.

Craziness and the delights of love.

51

Monday 16ᵗʰ August 2010

The MacKenzies, mother and daughter, gave me the warmest possible welcome last night.

Muriel held my hands in hers for a long time and gazed at me gratefully.

'All these years I'd been praying for a miracle,' she said, choking back a sob. 'I thought God had abandoned me. But now I know you're his miracle.'

It's obvious that Muriel is sick. She's clearly weak. She takes short steps and stops frequently to rest.

'It's the joy and the love that keep me going,' she says. 'Getting Julia back has done more for my health than all the cancer treatments.'

Julia is no less thankful. But I see no joy in her eyes.

She looks much better than she did when I found her three weeks ago at Gullinhamrar. She's sacrificed the red-brown hair that looked so beautiful in the pictures taken before she travelled to Iceland. It's cropped short. Almost like a boy's.

Sóley Árdís plays in the garden with Muriel when Julia asks me to come to her room.

It's spacious, with two big windows. There are no curtains.

'I feel I need to be able to see out, especially when I wake up in the night,' she says. 'If I don't see a window somewhere or an open door, the memories come flooding back, along with the horror of being locked up again.'

Julia wants me to hear about her nine-year nightmare.

'I couldn't tell Mum everything that happened,' she says. 'It's too horrible and she wouldn't be able to stand it.'

'It's also important to be able to speak openly with someone about such an ordeal.'

'I've given the police a detailed statement about my time in that dreadful place. I'm seeing a psychiatrist twice a week. But nobody else can understand what it was like to be those bastards' prisoner for nine years.'

Painful memories of my own struggle with brutal authority surface from the depths of my mind. Violence and threats. Incarceration and darkness.

Julia looks out of the window.

'I was so happy that July day in 2001,' she says. 'Everything had gone so well on the trip to the Highlands and I had met friendly and helpful people on the way. I was in seventh heaven.'

'Right up until you rode your bike up to Gullinhamrar?'

'I've wondered all these years if I could have done anything differently. When I told Jósteinn that Geiri had invited me to drop by, he was hospitable and offered to go out riding. There was nothing to indicate I had anything to fear. Quite the opposite. I could smell the alcohol, but Jósteinn just laughed it off and said that horses, booze and women were a holy trinity in Iceland.'

Julia gets to her feet. She goes over to the window.

'I often told myself while I was in captivity that he assaulted me because he was drunk, and that I should've known better than to go out riding with a drunk man. But I suspected nothing.'

'The assault wasn't your fault.'

'I know. But all the same…'

She doesn't finish her sentence.

'At first I thought he was going to kill me after the rape,' she continues after a long silence. 'He tied my hands behind my back with his whip and stuffed a filthy rag in my mouth. Then he started making calls on his mobile phone, furiously angry, but as if he had no idea what to do with me.'

'He was calling Alexander?'

'I suppose so. After that call he punched me hard with his fist and I was out cold.'

When Julia came to her senses, she expected her own death to be not far away.

'I was tied hand and foot, and there was tape over my mouth,' she said. 'I was given nothing to eat or drink for some days. I've no idea how many days as I lost all track of time after a while and was often half asleep or unconscious. They probably expected me to slip quietly into death, but the life force is strong, even under the worst imaginable conditions.'

She was alone in the tower for the first few days.

'I was losing it by the time they collected me in the dead of night,' she continues after a pause. 'They stripped off my clothes and put me in a bathtub, and brought me a white bathrobe before they bundled me back into the tower. Then they gave me bread and water that I wolfed down. I've never been so hungry and thirsty in my life.'

Julia gazes silently out of the window for a while.

'They said it was impossible for me to escape from the

tower because there were no doors or windows, and the walls were so thick that I could shout as loud as I liked and nobody would hear me. But I still tried to break through the door, and attacked Jósteinn when he came in. But he was always much stronger than I am.'

She comes back across to the bed and sits down.

'First it was just Jósteinn who came and raped me,' she says quietly. 'He was usually drunk when he came, and violent. I tried to resist, but he was much stronger so it was no use.'

'Understandably.'

'Gradually I got used to thinking about something else, something pleasant. Sometimes I could take my mind so completely elsewhere that it was as if I wasn't even there in the bed until he was long gone.'

She catches my eyes and continues.

'The worst was when he wanted me to enjoy being raped. I always said, "never, never" and then he'd be furiously angry and he'd beat me and yell "you want it, you bitch. You want it", as if he believed it himself.'

'Or he was trying to convince himself?' I say.

'Could be. Who knows how these sick bastards think?'

'What about Alexander?'

'He always brought food and took away the rubbish, but otherwise seemed to regard me as Jósteinn's property,' Julia answers. 'But that changed suddenly one day. He ordered me to strip off and raped me.'

'And continued to do so?'

'For a while he came more often than Jósteinn. Sometimes he wanted to tie me up first, as if he was concerned that I might escape. Unless he simply liked to tie women up.'

'You never got pregnant?'

Julia shakes her head.

'They always used condoms. Except for that first time,' she replies.

When our long conversation is over, we go together out into the garden. There's birdsong among the trees, but there's rain in the air.

'The nightmare of captivity follows me, awake and asleep,' Julia says. 'I wake up in the night, with those revolting men on top of me, and scream in hopeless desperation before I realise that I'm free.'

'I know from my own experience that the pain of the past

never leaves you,' I reply. 'But it's possible to soften it over time.'

'I bitterly regret the nine years of my life lost in that hell. Those were nine years I meant to use to educate myself and to work with nature and to spend with my mother. Those have been stolen from me and can't be reclaimed.'

'I know.'

'And I'm told that those animals won't even have to spend as long in prison as I spent locked up. Is that really true?'

'It's likely. If they behave themselves in prison.'

'Do you see that as justice?'

'Not in this case.'

'It makes me so angry, knowing those bastards will get off so lightly after their terrible crimes,' she says.

'Anger is a good place to start,' I say.

52

Thursday 19ᵗʰ August 2010

It's the first day back at work since Sóley Árdís and I returned to Iceland, and I go over the list of the legal practice's cases that Lísa Björk has been able to keep on the back burner while I was out of the country.

The District Court extended Markús Hálfdánarson's remand by a further two weeks while I was away in Florida. One of my first tasks this morning is to call the chief superintendent in Selfoss to find out if the boys in black have found Thorsteinn Rögnvaldsson's briefcase, or the manuscript that was certainly in his possession at Skálholt.

'This briefcase has unfortunately not been found,' Arnlaugur replies. 'We have searched extensively at Skálholt.'

'So it seems obvious that the murderer took the briefcase.'

'As you're aware, we also searched at Markús Hálfdánarson's home, with no success.'

'I'm referring to the real murderer.'

'Neither witness statements nor evidence indicate that anyone other than your client bears responsibility for this crime.'

Up to midday I clear up a bunch of minor cases, before it's time to meet Hallbera. This is the sister of Gunnsteinn Ástráðsson, the protestor with the red ring.

'She called twice from Raufarhöfn while you were away,' Lísa Björk says. 'The second time, I agreed to schedule a meeting with you.'

'That's fine. I'd like to meet her.'

We offer her a light lunch in the meeting room.

Hallbera is somewhere over fifty. She's tall and slim, with wavy brown hair. She's dressed in jeans and a colourful sweater.

'You found the girl at Gullinhamrar after everyone else had given up,' she says right away. 'That's why I called you. I've been holding out for news of my brother for thirty-seven years.'

'Did you provide a sample for the DNA analysis?'

'I did. But I can't believe that Gunnsteinn would have gone up there. He had no interest in walking in the Highlands.'

'I asked the police to check out that possibility.'

Hallbera looks at me in surprise.

'I had no idea,' she says. 'What made you think that might be an option?'

'This photo,' I say.

I place the picture borrowed from Thorsteinn Rögnvaldsson's museum in the Westman Islands on the table in front of her.

'As you can see there, Gunnsteinn's wearing a ring that's very noticeable,' I continue. 'It's very similar to the one I found up there on the Snæfellsnes glacier.'

She examines the picture carefully.

'They're all there, all the old comrades,' she says at last. 'Gunnsteinn, Ófeigur, Örnólfur, Thorsteinn and Símon.'

'You know them all by name?'

'Yes, I came to visit my brother two years running. First in 1972 and then again in 1973. Gunnsteinn rented a room from Örnólfur's parents on Lynghagi and I stayed with him, a fortnight each time. It was fun the whole time and they got up to all sorts of unbelievable stuff.'

'Such as what?'

'I was only fifteen and they smuggled me in to see *Hair* at Glaumbær. It was a sort of hippy thing, and the whole cast was naked at the end. I thought it was incredibly exciting.'

Hallbera opens a pink handbag that lies in her lap.

'I took some pictures on both trips.'

She hands me a small album. The first pictures are in black and white, and then some in colour.

The boys pose as a group for some of the pictures, and in others they're sitting around, drinking.

One picture shows just Gunnsteinn and Ófeigur.

They're sitting close together.

'Were they lovers?'

Hallbera doesn't reply straight away.

'They spent a lot of time together, Gunnsteinn and Ófeigur, but that was because they had shared interests,' she says at last. 'They were both getting to grips with art and poetry, and they both aimed high.'

'But that didn't happen, did it?'

'That's right. Gunnsteinn disappeared, and Ófeigur lost his way and gave up.'

'And there's a link between the two?'

'I don't think Ófeigur ever got over my brother's death.'

'He loved him so dearly?'

'Yes. All the talk about Gunnsteinn committing suicide hit him very hard, and he blamed himself.'

'In what way?'

'They came in for all kinds of abuse at nightclubs, and even on the street. Homosexuality was seen as something sick and disgusting at that time. Ófeigur was the one who'd initiated the relationship, so he felt a responsibility for what happened. But I told him that Gunnsteinn would never have taken his own life, and I still think so.'

Hallbera still hasn't touched her coffee.

'I was staying with him at Lynghagi when he disappeared,' she adds.

'Really?'

'He came home late that night and wasn't up until just before midday when his friends came to get him for a meeting.'

'Which friends?'

'Thorsteinn and Símon.'

'What sort of meeting?'

'That was all very vague. But I think they were going to prepare some kind of demonstration.'

'And Gunnsteinn went with them?'

'He did. Thorsteinn had a little blue Fiat and I saw it drive away. I watched from the window.'

'And you didn't see Gunnsteinn again after that?'

'No. He didn't come home that night. In the morning I asked Örnólfur if he knew where my brother was and he thought he'd been sent up to Akranes to paint some protest placards. That was the last his other friends knew of him. They said Gunnsteinn had taken the ferry to Akranes, but nobody over there recalled having seen him. That's why the rumours started to go around that he'd jumped overboard. I didn't believe it, but nobody listened to me.'

'So Thorsteinn and Símon were the last to see Gunnsteinn alive?'

'I don't know. They said they'd gone to that meeting with him and that afterwards Gunnsteinn had made his own way down to the harbour to catch the ferry. The police believed them.'

'And you don't?'

'I was only a youngster at the time, but I soon realised that the police had no real interest in finding Gunnsteinn,' she replies.

'But there was a search, to some extent? Wasn't there?'

'They had the beaches walked for a day, if I remember correctly. But that was all. At the same time, after a previous failure to solve a similar case, they were determined to treat another disappearance as murder, even though there was no more of a body in Gunnsteinn's case. They wouldn't accept that anything of that kind could have happened to my brother. It was as if they thought queers drowning themselves in Faxaflói was just fine.'

Hallbera looks at me in the eyes, questioningly.

'Do you really believe that Gunnsteinn could have gone up onto the glacier?'

'I've no idea,' I reply. 'But I felt this thing with the ring was too much of a coincidence to not follow it up.'

She nods her head.

'It seemed the right thing to do, to give the police a DNA sample when they asked for it,' she says. 'In the unlikely event that this turns out to be Gunnsteinn's remains, then I want you to be a hundred per cent clear in your mind that he'd never have gone of his own free will up onto a mountain like the Snæfellsnes glacier. I can assure you of that.'

'Understood.'

Hallbera finally turns to what's on the table, as if she's said everything she wants me to know.

'Have you been in touch with any of Gunnsteinn's old friends in recent years?' I ask.

'I ran into Ófeigur by chance at a teachers' conference last year. He said he had a few of my brother's paintings and offered to show them to me if I happened to be in the south. But that hasn't happened so far. We live a long way apart.'

'Did you get the feeling he's still mourning your brother?'

'Yes. It's just as well I'm not the only one.'

There's solace in shared sorrow, as Mother said.

53

After Hallbera leaves, I go carefully through her account.

What sticks in my mind is that she watched her brother leave on the day he disappeared.

Gunnsteinn was a passenger in Thorsteinn Rögnvaldsson's car. They were supposedly on their way to a meeting with comrades in the Movement.

Hallbera never saw him again.

Did the three of them turn up for this meeting?

Örnólfur Indriðason should know. If he was at that meeting as well.

I call him to find out and manage to get through. We arrange to meet again in the University of Reykjavík's canteen.

'I had a long and interesting conversation with Hallbera Ástráðsdóttir today,' I tell him as soon as we're both seated. 'She was at your house on Lynghagi the day Gunnsteinn disappeared.'

'That's right,' Örnólfur replies. 'The loss of her brother was a terrible shock for her.'

'She says that Thorsteinn Rögnvaldsson and Símon Andrésson picked Gunnsteinn up from the house on Lynghagi to take him to some meeting,' I continue. 'Were you also at that meeting?'

'No. I saw Gunnsteinn the previous evening, but not that day.'

'You remember this clearly? After thirty-seven years?'

'Gunnsteinn's suicide was an awful blow for all of us who knew him. For some days afterwards we could hardly speak of anything else, including where and when we'd last seen him. The police also asked about this, and those interrogations are still vivid in my memory.'

'What meeting was this?'

'I feel it's likely it was some working meeting to do with a possible protest.'

'But you don't know?'

Örnólfur shakes his head.

'Was Ófeigur Gunnarsson also at this meeting?'

'You'd have to ask him about that.'

'Do you know where he lives?'

'Yes. When Ófeigur called me unexpectedly last summer, he said that he'd been a teacher at Flúðir for some years. Up to that point, I hadn't heard from him since he went to art college abroad in the seventies.'

'So why did he call you?'

'He was wondering about former comrades in the Movement, and what had become of them.'

'Was he interested in anyone in particular?'

'No, I don't think so, as he asked about many of the people he hadn't seen for decades, and I told him what I knew about them. He seemed to be very interested in renewing their acquaintance.'

'Really?'

'Yes. That was very clear.'

'Have you spoken again?'

'I invited him to the seminar, as he lives at Flúðir, which isn't far from Skálholt. He arrived in time for my presentation and we had a long conversation afterwards.'

'Did he also meet Thorsteinn?'

'I brought them together, but I don't know if they had much of an opportunity to chat. As always, Thorsteinn had plenty of irons in the fire.'

'You could have mentioned that when we last spoke.'

Örnólfur shrugs.

'How could I have known you had an interest in Ófeigur Gunnarsson?' he asks with an irritated look on his face.

'It should have been obvious that I'm interested in everyone who met Thorsteinn at Skálholt, just a few hours before he was murdered.'

He takes my response badly. He gets quickly to his feet.

'So you're still trying to throw suspicion onto innocent people?' he rasps.

'No. Quite the opposite. I'm trying to save an innocent man.'

'Then leave Ófeigur in peace. He's already had more than his fair share of suffering in this life.'

I sit in thought at the table for a long time after Örnólfur has gone.

The question at the forefront of my mind is, *supposing there was no meeting of the Movement that day*?

I pull my smartphone from the pocket of my leather jacket. I call up the pictures I took in Rögnvaldur Rögnvaldsson's archive.

I read again his memo relating to Cussler and Gunnsteinn.

According to Rögnvaldur's notes, the US embassy requested

assistance in locating a young man who had taken valuable items from a US official staying at Hótel Loftleiðir. A second document indicates clearly that this official was Cussler.

At the bottom of the page Rögnvaldur had recorded indications from ThR and SA that Gunnsteinn Ástráðsson was the culprit.

'Relevant information been delivered into the right hands,' it says in red ink. My concern is that the final sentence says it all: *'SA brought them together. Case concluded.'*

If my suspicion is correct, Símon and possibly Thorsteinn took Gunnsteinn to meet Cussler on that fateful day in the summer of 1973, or else to meet some other secret service operative.

Then there's another question that's troubling me. What happened when Ófeigur Gunnarsson met Thorsteinn Rögnvaldsson for the first time in many years at the seminar at Skálholt? Could he have been given some kind of explanation of that last time Gunnsteinn, Thorsteinn and Símon got into the car together?

He alone knows the answer to that.

Ófeigur is also the only one who can tell me why he suddenly began looking back at the old days in the Movement.

I search the online phone directory. There's a home phone registered under Ófeigur Gunnarsson's name. I call and tell him I'd like to see him.

'What do you want from me?' he demands.

'I've had a long conversation with Hallbera Ástráðsdóttir,' I reply. 'I'd like to speak to you about her brother Gunnsteinn.'

'I have nothing to say to you about things that happened long ago.'

'Hallbera is still mourning her brother. It seems to me that you telling me about his final days is something she deserves.'

There's a long silence down the line.

'For Hallbera's sake, I'll meet you,' he says at last. 'But I have nothing new to tell you that she hasn't heard before.'

'I'll run up to Flúðir to see you on Monday.'

When I get back, Lísa Björk is about to leave the office.

'This arrived, recorded delivery,' she says.

I take the letter.

The sender is a research laboratory in Germany.

Sheesh!

It's the moment of truth – the reality of my daughter's paternity is about to be revealed.

54

Friday 20th August

Early in the morning I open the letter from the laboratory in Germany that compared my genetic sample to that of the Reverend Finnbogi.

I stare for a long time at the results.

Then I call the priest. I inform him that he's still childless.

The man of God refuses to believe me.

'You're welcome to take a look at the laboratory report at my office if you like,' I say. 'Apart from that, this matter is closed.'

Sóley Árdís remains fatherless.

I'm happy with that.

Símon Andrésson has no interest in meeting.

But I can't be bothered to listen to his mundane protestations of how terribly busy he is at the ministry.

'I'm calling you as Hallbera Ástráðsdóttir's lawyer,' I interrupt. 'She's asked me to look into the disappearance of her brother, Gunnsteinn Ástráðsson. As you're more aware than most people, he vanished in the summer of 1973 after getting into a car with you and Thorsteinn Rögnvaldsson. I need to ask you about that final car journey of Gunnsteinn's and I'd prefer to do this face to face than through the media.'

The silence on the line is a long one.

'Be here at three,' he says at last. 'I can postpone that meeting.'

He sits hunched and gloomy behind a vast desk. He's an overweight, besuited apparatchik whose cold reticence has no doubt put the fear of death into plenty of innocent minions.

'I don't appreciate threats,' he says.

'I haven't made any,' I shoot back. 'Not yet.'

'You insinuated during your call that I might have something to do with Gunnsteinn's tragic disappearance.'

'I was merely pointing out facts.'

'If you had familiarised yourself properly with the matter as a whole, you would be aware that Thorsteinn and I drove Gunnsteinn to a meeting that day and we parted there,' Símon says. 'Those were our only dealings with Gunnsteinn on the day he took his own life.'

'You're sticking to that story?'

'You dare to cast doubt on Thorsteinn's testimony?'

'Yes. Because I have indications to the contrary.'

'Indications?' he repeats. 'What indications?'

'I've seen a memo that indicates that on that day you two took Gunnsteinn to meet a US official who had a bone to pick with the lad.'

Símon glares at me from beneath heavy brows.

'I can't imagine that such a memo exists.'

'It does. I've read it.'

'Then show me.'

I shake my head.

'I'm happy to tell you that the memo is stored in a very safe place.'

He sits up straighter in his chair.

'I wanted to give you the opportunity to provide a correct and truthful version of what happened during that last car journey of yours and Gunnsteinn's,' I continue.

'This is impertinent and malicious supposition,' he says heavily. 'If you allow such allegations to appear publicly, then I'll make sure that you spend time in prison for libel and causing reputational damage.'

'So you're not going to tell me where or with whom you left Gunnsteinn that day?'

'We took him to a meeting to prepare a demonstration. Thorsteinn and I both gave statements to this effect in 1973. That was and remains the truth of the matter.'

I shrug.

'Fair enough.'

'If you had written evidence to the contrary at your disposal, then you wouldn't hesitate to show me.'

'I simply don't have formal permission to do so at this moment,' I reply. 'But I remember practically verbatim what's written in the memo dated June 1973. And it conflicts entirely with your story.'

Símon stares at me for a while.

'I heard a rumour recently that you're working for Rögnvaldur Rögnvaldsson,' he says after a long pause. 'Is that correct?'

I smile without saying anything.

'Would you like to change your story?'

He looks at me wordlessly. There's no mistaking that he's deep in thought.

'No. Let's just end this conversation,' he says and gets to his feet. 'I would urge you to bear my warning in mind.'

'You know what I know, and what I want,' I say as a parting shot.

I've no doubt that I've seriously disturbed Símon. He should know better than anyone that a great many old and uncomfortable secrets are hidden in Rögnvaldur Rögnvaldsson's archive at Thingvellir.

The question is, how will he react?

Hopefully, he'll think twice. But if it comes to down it, I can always fetch the documents and put them before a judge to support my case.

I'm certainly in a position to do this. At any rate, while Rögnvaldur is in a coma in hospital.

I'm on the way to the nursery when Máki calls.

'Did you see the press release from the National Commissioner of Police?' he asks.

'What press release?'

'About the arm you found up on the glacier?'

'There's a result?'

'Yep. They say that DNA analysis confirms that it's an Icelandic lad who disappeared in 1973.'

'Gunnsteinn Ástráðsson.'

Máki can't conceal his surprise.

'Yes, you already heard?'

'No, not at all. But I've suspected for a while that it's Gunnsteinn.'

'Tell me more.'

'I want to wait until after the weekend before saying anything more about this,' I tell him. 'But you could call Gunnsteinn's surviving sister to get her reaction.'

Sóley Árdís and I are just home when my phone plays its merry tune in my pocket.

'I've finished the first edit of our TV programme,' Rannveig says. 'I feel like inviting you and Sóley Árdís over for dinner and so we can watch it.'

'We'll be there around seven.'

I dress up as if for a Saturday night downtown. I put on scarlet underwear that's mostly transparent. Black leather skirt. White blouse. Black jacket.

I dab *Fleur de la Passion* behind each ear. *In Love Again*, it says on the bottle. That fits.

The TV programme about the glacier trip takes me by surprise. It's beautifully shot, and it's dramatic.

'Mum, you're so cool,' Sóley Árdís says when she sees me hurtle on the snowmobile across the white crust, dressed in polar explorer's heavy gear.

Afterwards we chat until Sóley Árdís starts to yawn.

'I got a special bed ready for you,' Rannveig says, getting to her feet. 'Would you like to see it?'

'Yes,' Sóley Árdís replies.

We follow Rannveig.

'This was my room when I was little,' she says.

My daughter sits on the bed.

'I want to sleep here,' she says.

'I bought you a toothbrush as well,' Rannveig says.

She's thought of everything.

'Shall I tell you a story?' I ask dutifully when Sóley Árdís is tucked up under the duvet.

She shakes her head.

'Sure, sweetheart?'

'Yep.'

I kiss her forehead.

'Aren't you going to cuddle as well?' Sóley Árdís asks.

Rannveig laughs gleefully.

'Absolutely,' she replies, and I kiss Sóley again. 'A cuddle is just what grown-ups need.'

55

Monday 23rd August 2010

Ófeigur Gunnarsson keeps me waiting.

An old lady living in the next house noticed my frustration. By then I've been sitting there in the silver steed for twenty minutes.

She takes me into her kitchen and puts coffee and biscuits on the table.

'I don't believe Ófeigur knows what punctuality is,' she says with a smile. 'He doesn't have a watch or a mobile phone, and pretty much lives in a world of his own, as I understand most of these artistic types do.'

With the coffee comes a generous helping of information. Among all this, I learn that Ófeigur has lived at Flúðir for eight years, and all that time has taught there at the junior school. He rents the old wooden house next door and uses the little lean-to garage as a workshop and studio. I also find out that he's eccentric, single and childless. He's also given to taking long walks around the district, sometimes in the middle of the night.

'At heart he's a lovely man,' she says. 'I hear that the children like him as a teacher.'

Ófeigur is tall and as thin as a rake. His red hair is long and dishevelled, as is only proper for an old hippie. The full beard is on the wild side.

He shows me into the basic studio in the garage. There's a chaos of paints, tubes, tins, brushes and other tools of the artist's trade on the bench at one side. Paintings large and small lean against the whitewashed wall.

I don't see a chair anywhere in this primitive workplace.

He goes to the door at the end of the garage. I follow through a utility room and from there down to a windowless cellar.

Down here there's a sort of sitting room. There's a yellow-upholstered sofa, a matching armchair, a circular coffee table and a small fridge.

Ófeigur ushers me to the armchair.

I'm facing a painting of a young, naked beau. He stares out of the canvas with a smile on his lips. I immediately recognise the look on his face from the photographs Hallbera showed me.

'That's Gunnsteinn, isn't it?' I ask.

'The Adonis of my youth,' Ófeigur replied in a voice full of emotion.

'You've heard the latest news?'

'They keep lying.'

'Who?'

'Gunnsteinn would never have gone up on the glacier to take his own life.'

'You're certain of that?'

'I am.'

'All the same, it's a relief for Hallbera to know what became of her brother.'

His dark brown eyes glare at me.

'She knows?'

'It is at any rate clear where his final resting place is. That's even though there's still no explanation of why Gunnsteinn ended up on the Snæfellsnes glacier.'

'Precisely.'

'Do you know?'

'Me?'

'Yes. You were his closest friend.'

'You're on the wrong track.'

Ófeigur goes over to the fridge and takes out a glass bottle that's half-full of some liquid.

I glance again at the painting of Gunnsteinn while Ófeigur pours into glasses.

He finally sits back down on the sofa and hands me one glass. It appears to be acceptably clean.

'Do you remember who said that wine is the pinnacle of civilisation?' he asks.

I shake my head.

'It doesn't matter. The words live on, while people die.'

He empties his glass in one swallow.

'Knock it back in one,' he says. 'Otherwise this visit is at an end.'

I make myself do it. The drink tastes foul.

'Did you meet Gunnsteinn on the day he disappeared?'

'No.'

'So you weren't at this meeting with him?'

'There was no meeting.'

'Thorsteinn Rögnvaldsson and Símon Andrésson both gave statements to the police, setting out that they drove him to a meeting on that day.'

Ófeigur snorts.

'I've never come across anyone who remembers being at that particular meeting.'

'Örnólfur Indriðason told me that you called him in the summer, for the first time in decades, to ask about former comrades from the Movement. Why now, after all these years?'

'Don't you know?'

'No.'

'Weren't you the one who found the ring up on the glacier?'

'Yes, of course.'

'I recognised it from the pictures in the papers.'

'Gunnsteinn's ring?'

'That was when I knew he was deep in the glacier, and that everyone had lied.'

'Aha!'

'It was all because of Thorsteinn,' he continues.

'How do you know that?'

'Because he was an agent of the enemy. That was why Gunnsteinn disappeared into that black hole that never returns what it catches.'

'Did Thorsteinn admit in your hearing that he'd betrayed Gunnsteinn to this enemy? I mean, when you met him at Skálholt?'

'He played the part of being our friend and colleague. But his whole life had been an endless litany of betrayal, lies and deception. Those were his own words.'

'He said that to you?'

'I read it myself.'

'Where?'

'Thorsteinn was writing a book about his life of betrayal.'

'You've seen the manuscript?'

'I went to Thorsteinn's room while he was pursuing a woman, and saw the book where he had written in black and white that he'd always been a liar and a traitor.'

Aha!

'What was your reaction?'

'I finally understood how everything fitted, how everything has a beginning and an end, origins and effects, how all these things hang together and there's no such thing as coincidence, how what I have to do is an inevitable consequence of what others did long ago. It was a wonderful revelation.'

I'm starting to feel very strange.

Ófeigur looks at me with a peculiar smirk on his face.

I try to get to my feet, but I can't. My body absolutely refuses to obey do as it's told.

I realise that the old bastard has slipped me some kind of roofie.

The manic grin on his face confirms my fear.

Fucking hell!

56

I can feel the cool breeze playing over my face.

The wind's cold breath is the first thing I sense after the dark nightmare of unconsciousness.

Where am I?

Right in front of me a deep chasm yawns open. The churning grey-green torrent batters the rock sides, hurrying as if in a wild game of chase.

I don't know this place – never been here before.

Ófeigur Gunnarsson stands behind me.

I sense his presence before catching sight of him. I can also sense that he's dangerous. Not that I recall right away quite why.

He snatches hold of my arm, hard.

'You don't fool me,' he whispers in my ear.

I try to reply, but it's difficult to get words out.

'What do you want?' I stammer at last.

'Peace and freedom,' he replies. 'Peace and the freedom to enjoy my revenge.'

I glance down. I look down from the precipice into the maelstrom far below my feet.

'You can have all the peace you want as far as I'm concerned,' I tell him.

'You're lying, just like all the others, but I've given up listening to liars.'

I feel that the shackles of the drug he must have sneaked into my drink are starting to loosen.

'If you hurt me, you'll get neither peace nor freedom.'

'I'm happy to deal with one problem at a time.'

'Many people know I was coming to see you. They'll call the police if I don't get in touch with the office.'

'Lies and more lies.'

He takes a deep breath, as if he's preparing himself for action.

My reaction is pure instinct.

I drop to my knees just as he pushes with both hands against my back.

He's not prepared for that. He loses his balance and falls forward over me.

Ófeigur falls head first onto the rough cliff edge. His hands are outstretched as he lurches forward. He manages to catch hold of me with one hand.

I'm lying face down, fingers scratching a hold on the coarse rock.

But there's some weight to Ófeigur, and he's not letting go his grip.

He pulls me with him over the edge and into the chasm.

We land hard on the wet boulders.

He first, then me.

I crash onto him, which softens my landing.

For a while I lie dazed on top of him.

The wild waves of the river spray me like a downpour. But they aren't able to snatch us away into the flood.

I sit up and push myself against the rock wall. With my fingers I wipe the water from my face, and look down at Ófeigur, lying on his back.

His blue overalls are soaked, and not just with water.

Those red stains can't be anything but blood.

The old man's not moving. But his eyes are open.

'You were too quick for me,' he says with surprise in his voice.

'Where are we?'

'This is the holiest cathedral of the Hvít river.'

'And what's it called?'

'Brúarhlöð.'

I find my phone in my jacket pocket. To my relief it wasn't smashed in the fall. I call the emergency services and tell them that the two of us have tumbled into the Hvít river at Brúarhlöð.

'We need police and an ambulance immediately!' I yell.

Ófeigur coughs up blood.

'I reckon you're dead meat,' I say.

He wipes his mouth with the back of his hand.

'Not before time,' he answers.

The old guy licks his bloody lips.

'Do you know the highest duty we Nordic people have?'

'No.'

'It's the obligation to seek vengeance for our loved ones.'

I set the phone recording. I can see his face on the screen.

'Don't you think it's fitting to make a historical record of your achievements?' I add. 'While you still can?'

'I'm satisfied that I avenged Gunnsteinn, even though it

took such a long time.'

'Tell me about it.'

'I believed that Gunnsteinn had taken his own life in Faxaflói, as everyone said he had, even though his sister refused to believe it. But when I saw the picture of the ring, I knew it had to be a lie. Gunnsteinn would never have gone up onto the glacier of his own free will, and certainly not without telling me.'

He coughs again. Then wipes more blood from his lips.

'Örnólfur put me on the track,' he continues. 'He reminded me that Thorsteinn and Símon had collected Gunnsteinn that day from Lynghagi. I paid Símon a visit and he told me that Thorsteinn on his own had taken Gunnsteinn to his destination.'

'He said that?'

'Yes. But Thorsteinn didn't recall that. Imagine it, he didn't remember having betrayed Gunnsteinn that day, with a smile on his face.'

'Tell me how Thorsteinn died.'

'I knew where he was and went out into the night with a golf club that I picked up in the lobby, and smashed his traitorous head. After that, I went out onto the pasture, lay in the grass and found – at long, long last – some peace of mind.'

'But why did Jónína Katrín also have to die?'

Ófeigur again licks the blood from his lips.

'I was overwhelmed by the fury of righteous revenge,' he says. 'I let fall blow after blow as he lay on top of the woman and that's why she got the same treatment. They were together in peace and death.'

I stop the recording. The phone gets tucked away in my pocket. I wait impatiently for the ambulance, cold and wet under the spray of the churning river.

Ófeigur closes his eyes. But he's still drawing breath.

Despite all this, I hope the old guy survives, so he can tell his story in court.

Otherwise, the dying declaration recorded on my phone will have to serve to convince the city's finest of my client's innocence.

57

Friday 27th August 2010

The Selfoss police meticulously examined my phone recording of Ófeigur Gunnarsson's confession. They couldn't question the man himself. He breathed his last in the ambulance on the way to hospital.

All the same, Arnlaugur clearly has his doubts about my account of events. That was right up to when they found Thorsteinn Rögnvaldsson's briefcase when Ófeigur's house at Flúðir was searched.

'In spite of everything, it seems that you were right about the murders at Skálholt,' the chief superintendent admitted with reluctance last Tuesday. 'That means that your client has no case to answer.'

Markús Hálfdánarson has kept his head down since his release.

I collected him from Litla Hraun. Then drove him home to Seltjarnarnes where Rannveig was waiting for him.

She turned away when he reached out to embrace her.

Together we knocked up a brief statement in which Markús Hálfdánarson welcomed the lifting of the charges wrongly placed against him. He thanked all those who had made efforts to prove his innocence.

'My hope is that this is the last time that anyone in Iceland is held in isolation for months on end for a crime they did not commit,' he stated in conclusion.

The city's finest have remained tight-lipped in public about how this case has been concluded. They simply state that Ófeigur confessed before his death to the murders at Thorláksbúð, and that items supporting this confession were found at his home.

Not that this stopped Máki asserting that the murder of Thorsteinn Rögnvaldsson was linked to the disappearance of Gunnsteinn Ástráðsson in 1973.

The *News Blog* sets the tone:

Nixon's arrival – Gunnsteinn's disappearance

The old newshound alleges that Gunnsteinn's disappearance can be linked to the arrival of US spy John Adam Cussler, who came to Iceland shortly before US President Nixon arrived for a meeting in Reykjavík with the President of France on 31st May 1973. All the indications are that Cussler had been the original owner of the *Ring of Death* that was found on the finger of the dead Movement comrade up on the glacier.

He still takes care not to go so far as to insinuate that the US secret services could be behind Gunnsteinn's death. But it's there between the lines.

Máki published an extensive interview with Hallbera Ástráðsdóttir in which she confirmed that her brother and Ófeigur Gunnarsson were very close friends. She recounted what she knew of the last days of her brother's life, including that final car journey with his comrades, Thorsteinn Rögnvaldsson and Símon Andrésson.

Following the publication of the interview, Símon released a short statement, reiterating his previous account of that car journey.

On Hallbera's behalf, I presented a written formal request for a special police inquiry into her brother's disappearance and death. I'm not optimistic that the boys in black will go along with that. But I'll keep up the pressure on the jobsworths in the hope of beating them into submission.

The old newshound is pretty sure he knows what happened. Not that he dares say so on *News Blog*.

'My guess is that they interrogated Gunnsteinn at the military base at Keflavík, and then took him up in a helicopter over the glacier,' he said when he called at lunchtime.

'And just let him drop?'

'That was their standard practice in Vietnam and South America at that time when they wanted people to disappear.'

Sóley Árdís and I are loading the dishwasher after dinner when the phone rings.

'Símon got in touch again this afternoon,' Máki says.

The Justice Ministry's evil apparatchik has made repeated attempts to get Máki to confirm that I was his source for the story.

'He didn't make an outright threat, but he made it clear that for the next few weeks or months, both of us are going to be watched very carefully.'

'So do take care.'

'Yep. Will do.'

'You know that Símon knows better than almost anyone

how to manipulate the power system behind the scenes. We can expect to be ambushed, from unexpected directions and without warning.'

'I know.'

It's not long before the phone rings again.

'I feel like going up to Thingvellir and trying to take it easy for the weekend,' Rannveig says.

'How are you feeling?'

'It's been a stormy few days. But there's a conclusion. Markús will stay here until he's found himself an apartment. I'm filing for divorce after the weekend and he's promised not to contest it.'

'Good for you.'

'But now I need to relax for a few days and rebuild my energy levels in the countryside,' Rannveig continues. 'Are you coming as well?'

What else?

Love is an inexhaustible source of dreams and hopes, as Mother said.

58

Saturday 28th August 2010

We hurtle in the silver steed past Gljúfrasteinn and up onto Mosfellsheiði.

Rannveig is in the back of the car with my daughter. She's determined to leave all the worries and problems of the last few days behind in the shadows of the city.

'I want to sit in the garden in the fine weather, play in the grass with our child and just enjoy being,' she said with a warm smile.

Our child?

Her words convey the promise of an even closer relationship. If I want and if I can.

The Thingvellir district is bright and beautiful in all the range of colours of autumn that nature knows is almost here.

I drive along the gravel track that leads down to the water. Home to Himinbjörg.

I pull up a little way short of the parking spaces.

The black jeep is exactly where Rögnvaldur Rögnvaldsson left it, the day the ambulance whisked him away to the National Hospital in Reykjavík.

But next to it is another car. A white Audi.

'Expecting visitors?' I ask.

'No,' Rannveig replies.

'Then we have an uninvited guest. Do you recognise the car?'

'No.'

I park the silver steed right behind the white car.

'He's not getting away without our say-so,' I say.

We go into the garden and look around carefully.

There's no unexpected visitor to be seen.

'How many people have keys to the house?' I ask.

'Now it's just me and my grandfather,' Rannveig replies. 'I have my dad's set of keys.'

'And I left your grandfather's keys in the bag he took with him to the hospital.'

I lead Sóley Árdís to the table in the garden.

'Now you have to stay here with Rannveig,' I tell her.

'Why?'

'Because what Mum says, goes.'

'All right.'

Rannveig sits at the table with my daughter in her arms. She hands me the keys to the house.

The light in the hall is on.

I know for certain that I switched the light off before I locked the house, when the ambulance rushed Rögnvaldur to Reykjavík.

Absolutely certain.

I look first in the kitchen but see no evidence of anyone having been there.

I go to the living room.

There's a little black bag on the coffee table.

It's open.

I look inside it and see right away that this is Rögnvaldur's bag. It's the one that was in the drawer of the table beside his hospital bed.

How did that come to be here?

I turn the possibilities over in my mind. Then I make my cautious way back to the hall where I'd noticed Rögnvaldur's golf bag. I take a club.

It pays to be cautious.

I go straight to the library with the club in both hands. I notice immediately that the corner cabinet has been moved.

But the door to the archive itself is locked.

I lean the club up against the wall. I faultlessly tap in the code numbers, one after another. Then I hear the low click as it opens.

There's a strange smell coming along the passage.

I hesitate. Then I pull the door open.

I'm met by the harsh smell of smoke. It's strong and vile.

Back up the steps in a rush and I make for the bathroom. I turn on the shower, grab a large towel and wet it thoroughly under the flow of water.

Then I hurry back down the steps. The wet towel's covering my mouth and nose. I draw a deep breath. Then I look around the doorway. I turn on more lights. I look around quickly.

Many of the filing cabinets are open.

In the far corner is a pile of half-burned folders.

Someone has piled up the secret files against the wall and set fire to them.

212

I pause to think for a moment, and run back up the steps and to the living room. I take one of the dining chairs back down with me. This wedges the door of the archive open. I don't want to risk the door closing while I'm inside the smoke-filled room.

I draw another deep breath. Holding the towel tight to my face, I go quickly into Rögnvaldur Rögnvaldsson's archive.

There are dozens of folders piled in the corner. Could be hundreds. Some are badly burned, others less so.

Behind the filing cabinet against the far wall lies a man in a suit.

Símon Andrésson.

The horror of death is chiselled into the lawyer's face.

His mouth is wide open, eyes staring.

Rögnvaldur's words come back to me.

'The computer is also programmed to react if a fire were to break out. It will lock the archive instantly, stopping the flow of oxygen and extinguishing the fire.'

I hurry back up the steps, out into the sunshine in the garden. I call the emergency line.

It's almost five in the afternoon by the time the city's finest have finished. They've taken statements from me and Rannveig. They've photographed and examined the scene of the fatality in the basement. They've checked out the archive's automatic fire extinguisher system. They've taken Símon Andrésson's body away.

They seal the archive.

Rannveig's giving my daughter something to eat in the kitchen.

'I've known for a long time that my grandfather kept a lot of old secrets in that archive of his,' she says. 'But it never occurred to me that they could be so dangerous.'

'Símon was undoubtedly concerned that I might be able to make them initiate a new investigation into Gunnsteinn Ástráðsson's disappearance,' I reply. 'Your grandfather's files indicate that Símon played a part in that. So that's why he tried to destroy them.'

'And Dad? Did he bear any responsibility for that young man's fate?'

'Símon told Ófeigur Gunnarsson that Thorsteinn drove Gunnsteinn to the last destination. But your grandfather's files indicate that it was Símon who did that.'

'I see.'

'It seems to me that this lie of Símon's led directly to Ófeigur attacking your father at Skálholt. Símon is indirectly responsible not just for Gunnsteinn's death, but also for the murders at Skálholt.'

Rannveig shudders.

'I can't stay here,' she says.

'All right.'

'And I don't want to go straight home.'

'Then we can find a hotel instead,' I reply, and fetch my phone.

Half an hour later we leave Himinbjörg behind, heading for the bucolic tranquillity of Borgarfjörður. That's in the hope of being able to forget the pain of everything that has gone on.

As the silver steed heads off into the sunset, Sóley Árdís and Rannveig break into song together on the back seat.

Song is the straightest route to the heart, as Mother said.